THE
PINE
ISLANDS

MARION POSCHMANN

TRANSLATED BY JEN CALLEJA

THE
PINE
ISLANDS

COACH HOUSE BOOKS | TORONTO

LIBRARY AND ARCHIVES CANADA CATALOGUING IN PUBLICATION

Title: The pine islands / Marion Poschmann ; translated by Jen Calleja.

Other titles: Kieferninseln. English

Names: Poschmann, Marion, 1969- author. | Calleja, Jen, translator.

Description: Translation of: Die Kieferninseln. | English translation originally published: London: Serpent's Tail, 2019.

Identifiers: Canadiana (print) 20200157213 | Canadiana (ebook) 20200157221 | ISBN 9781552454015 (softcover) | ISBN 9781770566378 (PDF) | ISBN 9781770566286 (EPUB)

Classification: LCC PT2676.O729 K5413 2019 | DDC 833/.92—dc23

The Pine Islands is available as an ebook: ISBN 978 1 77056 628 6 (EPUB), ISBN 978 1 77056 637 8 (PDF)

Purchase of the print version of this book entitles you to a free digital copy. To claim your ebook of this title, please email sales@chbooks.com with proof of purchase. (Coach House Books reserves the right to terminate the free digital download offer at any time.)

Go to the pine if you want to learn about the pine.
— Matsuo Bashō

TOKYO

He'd dreamt that his wife had been cheating on him. Gilbert Silvester woke up distraught. Mathilda's black hair lay spread out on the pillow next to him, tentacles of a malevolent pitch-black jellyfish. Thick strands of it gently stirred in time with her breathing, creeping toward him. He quietly got out of bed and went into the bathroom, where he stared aghast into the mirror. He left the house without eating breakfast. When he finished work that evening he still felt dumbfounded, almost numb. The dream hadn't dissipated over the course of the day and hadn't faded sufficiently for the inane expression 'dreams are but shadows' to be applicable. On the contrary, the night's impressions had become steadily stronger, more conclusive. An unmistakable warning from his unconscious to his naive, unsuspecting ego.

He walked into the hallway, dropped his briefcase theatrically, and confronted his wife. She denied everything. This only confirmed his suspicions. Mathilda seemed different. Unusually fervent. Agitated. Ashamed. She accused him of slipping out early in the morning without saying goodbye. I. Was. Worried. How. Could. You. Endless accusations. A flimsy deflection tactic. As if the blame suddenly lay with him. She had gone too far. He wouldn't allow it.

He couldn't recall later on whether he had shouted at her (probably), struck her (surely not), or spat at her (well, really, a little spittle may very well have sprayed from his mouth while he was talking animatedly at her), but he had, at any rate, gathered a few things together, taken his credit cards and his passport, and left, walking along the pavement past the house, and when she didn't come after him and didn't call out his name, he carried on, somewhat slower at first and then faster, till he reached the next underground station and disappeared down the steps, one might say in hindsight, as if sleepwalking. He travelled through the city and didn't get out until he reached the airport.

He spent the night in Terminal B, uncomfortably sprawled across two metal chairs. He kept checking his smart phone. Mathilda hadn't sent him any messages. His flight was leaving the next morning, the earliest intercontinental flight he could book at short notice.

In the plane en route to Tokyo he drank green tea, watched two samurai films, and repeatedly reassured himself that he had not only done everything right, but that his actions had indeed been inevitable, were still inevitable, and would carry on being inevitable, not only according to his personal opinion, but according to world opinion.

He'd retreat. He wouldn't insist on his rights. He'd make way, for whomever it was. Her boss, the head teacher, a grouchy macho kind of guy. The handsome adolescent she was allegedly mentoring, a trainee teacher. Or one of those pushy women she teaches with. He was no match for a woman. With a man, time would potentially be on his side. He could wait and see how things developed, ride out the storm until she changed her mind. It stood to reason that the allure of what was forbidden would fade sooner or later. But up against another woman he didn't stand a chance. Unfortunately, the dream hadn't been completely clear on this point. Overall, however, the dream had been clear enough. Very clear. As if he had suspected it. He had essentially suspected it. For quite a while actually. Hadn't she been in a remarkably good mood for the last few weeks? Down-right cheerful? And markedly friendly toward him? A diplomatic kind of friendliness that had grown more and more unbearable as time went on, which would have become even more unbearable if he had known what was hiding behind it sooner. But this was how she had managed to lull him into a false sense of security for so long. And he had allowed himself to be lulled, a clear failure on his part. He'd dropped his guard, allowed himself to be disappointed, because his suspicion hadn't been limitless.

The Japanese flight attendant, long black hair put up in a knot, presented him tea with a dazzling smile. Of course, her smile wasn't for him personally, but it soothed his entire body, as if someone had poured a bucket of balm over him. He sipped his tea and saw that she maintained this smile as she made her way through the cabin, that she bestowed it on each and every one of the passengers, immutable, a masklike grace that fulfilled its purpose with unsettling efficiency.

He'd always feared that he was too boring for Mathilda. From the outside, their relationship seemed in good order. But he couldn't offer her much in the long run, no dynamic social life, no astounding her with his wit, no depth of character.

He was a humble researcher, an associate lecturer. He hadn't made it to professor because he lacked the proper family background; he didn't know how to make useful contacts, he didn't know how to schmooze, he couldn't sell himself. He'd realized far too late that the world of the university was primarily about exercising power in a hierarchical system, and that the matter at hand was only of secondary or tertiary importance. This was where he had made an error, a myriad of errors. He'd criticized his doctoral supervisor. He'd always known better at the most inappropriate moment. Then, intimidated, held back just when he should have been bragging.

As a thick blanket of cloud passed by beneath him, the years drifted by in his memory, a gloomy grey mass of indignities and failures. As a young man, he had believed that he was of superior intelligence, that he stood out from the crowd of stuffy, well-adjusted overachievers, and that he would cut through the affairs of the world with philosophical ingenuity. Now he found himself once more in precarious circumstances, making his way from one project to the next, and saw himself professionally left in the dust by former friends who had all got vastly worse marks than he had and who had never expressed a single innovative idea between them. Friends who, to be blunt, were technically less competent than he was. But unlike him they possessed that certain clever demeanour, the kind that was the only valuable thing when it came to careers.

While they were settling down in their own homes with their families and routines, he saw himself forced into carrying out idiotic and meagrely remunerated work imposed on him by people he categorically despised. For years he had lived in fear of this kind of work so overcoming him that he could no longer think clearly. Then the fear had subsided and had given way to a feeling of general apathy. He carried out what was asked of him, turned his keen senses to the foolhardiest of tasks, and, in the meantime, alas years or decades too late, became able to give the impression that he was fine with everything, that he wasn't against it, but for it.

The Japanese flight attendant came by with a basket, steam rising from it. She passed him a hot, rolled-up flannel with a pair of long metal tongs. He mechanically wiped his hands with it, wrung the flannel around his wrists, let the stinging heat penetrate his pulse, this custom is such a respite, he thought, a peculiar flight where everyone was doing their utmost to keep him calm, he ran the flannel over his forehead, a motherly hand during a fever, incredibly pleasant, but it had already started to cool, he lay it over his face, only a couple of seconds, until it was nothing more than a cold, damp cloth.

His current work had made him an expert in beard styles. Though unrivalled in the dubiousness stakes, it had at least secured him a steady income over the years. And over time he had succeeded in finding enjoyment in this ineffable subject, which was incidentally the way it always went – that the interest in the individual parts grew the more one was immersed in the whole system. At the driving school he had enthused over the highway code, at the dance school over step sequences; it wasn't rocket science or witchcraft to have the ability to identify with something.

Gilbert Silvester, beard researcher in the context of a third-party project sponsored primarily by the North Rhine-Westphalian film industry, and secondarily by a feminist organization in Düsseldorf and the Jewish community in Cologne.

The project examined the impact of the representation of beards in film. It incorporated aspects of cultural studies, gender theory, and religious iconography, and it queried the possibility of philosophical expressivity via the medium of the image.

As always it was a research project where the results had already been established. He carried out the legwork, amassed the minutiae, confirmed through the richness of the material its significance, attested to the general applicability of its cultural theoretical conclusions, and revealed, finally and not without flourish, the surprising conclusions, which in reality were not only not all that surprising but had in fact been present in Gilbert's mind from the very beginning, and ultimately had vanishingly little impact on the film industry's immense power to manipulate viewers around the world.

He went to the library in the mornings, would turn off his mobile phone and sink into reproductions of the Italian masters, into mosaics and book illustrations from the Middle Ages. Depictions of beards were ubiquitous, and he had long wondered how it could be that such a fundamental issue hadn't been researched a long time ago. *Beard fashions and the image of God* was his thematic focal point, which, depending on the day, he found either enormously fruitful, electrifying even, or completely absurd and deeply depressing.

As the last bastion of his personal resistance, he had held on to certain nostalgic habits from his schooldays. Notes handwritten only with a fountain pen and ink, in black notebooks bound with thread. A leather satchel darkened over the course of decades, never a nylon backpack. A shirt and jacket at all times. These had helped him make an impression as a student and maintain his position as the most sensitive of intellectuals. Now these idiosyncrasies were simply further manifestations of his downfall. He clung to words that had long fallen out of usage and to implements of a past age – there was something anti-quated about him. Indeed, he had tried to offset it with post-modern ties and neon-coloured pocket squares. To no avail. He was regarded at the university as a reactionary aesthete. Ciga-rette smoke brought on headaches. He didn't care for soccer, and he didn't eat meat.

He wiped his palms again, spread out the white terrycloth square on his fold-down table, and left it like that.

Beneath him the blanket of cloud tore open and allowed a glimpse of Siberia. The mighty Ob River with its many streams nobly snaked its way through the swamplands and forests. On the screen the dummy airplane fitfully moved a little away from Tomsk in the direction of Krasnoyarsk and further on toward Irkutsk.

European Russia, Siberia, Mongolia, China, Japan – a flight path that only passed over tea-drinking nations. Until now, Gilbert Silvester had categorically dismissed countries with above-average tea consumption. He travelled in coffee-drinking countries, France, Italy, he enjoyed ordering a café au lait after a museum visit in Paris or requesting a café crème in Zurich; he liked Viennese coffee houses and the entire cultural tradition tied to it. A tradition of visibility, of being present, of clarity. In coffee countries things are overt. In tea countries everything is played out under a shroud of mysticism. In coffee countries one is able to buy things, revel in selective luxury even with the most modest financial resources. In tea countries one can only acquire the same with the power of the imagination. He would never have willingly travelled to Russia, a country that urges its people to imagine the basic needs of everyday life into existence, even just a cup of ordinary ground coffee. With the fall of the wall East Germany, to its delight, changed from a tea to a coffee state.

But he, Gilbert Silvester, had been forced by his own wife to travel to an avowed nation of tea. He was even willing to consider this Japan – with its gruellingly lengthy, exceptionally detailed, indeed devastatingly pretentious tea culture – as the most extreme level of tea country, and so all the more excruciating for him, all the more sadistic of Mathilda to think it was reasonable to make him do this. But he was not going to hold back any longer, he was going there, out of pure freedom, out of spite.

He took his smart phone out of his breast pocket and checked for messages. Then he realized that he must have put it on flight mode and that messages were unlikely to arrive for the time being. He opened his mailbox anyway, and, in spite of this, he was disappointed not to find anything. He didn't feel well. He was a little nauseous, from the air, from the tea on an empty stomach. He hadn't eaten in over thirty hours, to be exact. A sign of regret from Mathilda's side would have been normal. A polite enquiry, a minimal attempt at contact. But he had received nothing. Had Mathilda lost her mind? Why was she no longer familiar with the fundamental constants of interpersonal relations? Why had she let it get to the point where he saw himself obliged to go on an international escapade, right over Siberia? He felt the green tea lying heavily in his stomach and sloshing with every jolt of the aircraft.

He didn't know a great deal about Japan – it wasn't exactly the land of his dreams. During the samurai era, the country had banished its unpopular intellectuals to remote islands or forced them to carry out seppuku, a gory form of suicide. The way things were going, he was travelling to the right place.

He played another samurai film but didn't watch it. He spent the remaining flight time in an arduous semi-conscious state. He only vaguely comprehended his surroundings, blanking out the other passengers. Everything seemed indistinct to him, as if cloaked in thick fog, only this fog was bearing down on him and he had to use all his strength not to be smothered by it. He tensed his shoulders, his neck, he was Atlas slowly petrifying.

He couldn't manage even a minute of sleep.

After landing he retrieved his messages, but no one had contacted him. Term hadn't started yet, he wouldn't be neglecting any appointments in the coming weeks, and no one from the university would miss him. Lectures didn't begin again until the end of October. Until then, he only had to present a lecture at a conference in Munich. He had cancelled his attendance even before his luggage arrived on the carousel.

He exchanged some money and bought a travel guide and a couple of Japanese classics in English translation from a newsagent. The works of Bashō, *The Tale of Genji*, *The Pillow Book*. He had always assumed that he, like everyone else, knew the Japanese classics off by heart, but standing in front of the shelf with the pocket books, he now had to admit that he himself had at most watched a couple of Japanese films during his life-time and had never been able to so much as recite a haiku.

He stowed the books in his leather satchel and took the airport shuttle, the Narita Express, into the centre of Tokyo. From Tokyo Central Station he took a taxi to his hotel. It was all so easy. He had travelled halfway around the world as if on autopilot, no obstacles, no delays, no problems. The taxi driver wore white gloves and a uniform with a peaked cap and shiny buttons. He couldn't speak English but nodded knowledgeably when Gilbert showed him the piece of paper with the address on it. The journey went by in complete silence, which Gilbert found agreeable. The car glided along the road like a cross between a wedding cake and a Princess Barbie carriage, its seats covered with white crocheted lace. There were no traffic jams or red lights, no other cars, no outside world. When they pulled up, the driver handed him his luggage while enthusiastically bowing. A glass door slid aside noiselessly.

His room, a white box, was practically empty. It comprised a white bed with a white bedspread, and there were two white cubes on the floor that were evidently supposed to be furniture. Very modest, very modern. He stood in the middle of the room for a while with absolutely no idea what he was doing there. Then he lay on the bed and fell straight to sleep.

Dreams of what remained from the day. Tea nations, samurai. The swordfighter dresses himself in silken garments for a crucial battle and he pays the tea master a visit. He strides over the polished stepping stones toward the tea hut hidden behind a bamboo screen in the tiny garden, he has to stoop to get through the much too small door, almost crawling before the tea master. The tea master says a few words, whisks the tea to a froth, passes it to the guest, and the guest has the chance, before his not improbable death, to look upon the flower arrangements and the scroll painting with its precious calligraphy, he has the chance to lose himself in the room where the erratic shadows of the plants tumble in, where a breathtaking silence prevails.

The next morning he girds himself and heads into battle. He wields mystical powers; not only does his sword move as if of its own volition, but he can also fly, while others are only able to jump at best. These abilities have earned him the reputation of being an invincible sword master, but the opposing side outnumbers them, and his party is defeated. Filled with sorrow, he soars over the battlefield, sees all of the unnaturally twisted bodies that he cannot save, leaves them behind, and rises higher, until he can see the sea shimmering in the distance. Japan from above, the countless islands, thickly forested mountains, a sumptuous green lapped at by this stirring, solemn blue, he flies over the gruesome beauty of this country one final time before taking his short sword and, as tradition demands, slitting open his stomach.

Gilbert Silvester had seen the Japanese islands from above during the incoming flight, in the light of the setting sun, and in truth this sight had momentarily overwhelmed him. Now he awoke in a bare hotel room he didn't recognize. Where did both of these knee-high cubes – which seemed to be of absolutely no use whatsoever – come from? Were they in case of a brief fainting spell in a fitness studio? Or maybe an ice cube advertisement, which, to his own surprise, he had some-how fallen into? Had he recently been shooting TV commer-cials somewhere in the depths of his unconscious? He stepped toward the floor-length window, pulled across the ice-white curtain, and looked at the towering glass facade of Tokyo. How had he ended up in this city without the slightest effort? What did he want to do here? The mirrored glass of the building opposite sent flashes of light into his eyes, and he had to blink intensely; reflective blue glass floor after floor, dismissive, cool. What should he do here? He was, he suddenly put it to himself, very far from everything that had ever been familiar to him. He had taken himself off into the unknown, into this most unfamiliar of environments, and the eerie feeling he was expe-riencing stemmed from the fact that this environment didn't seem eerie in the slightest, simply functional, somewhat pretentious, and somewhat sterile. He showered, put on a fresh shirt, and took the lift twenty-four floors down.

It was early evening, the air was still warm, the first lights were coming on in the open-plan offices. Gilbert ambled along the busy streets and allowed himself to be compelled over huge crossings at intersections with the Japanese workforce clocking off for the day. He would have liked to have bought himself something to eat, but he felt too porous to make a decision, indeed, he felt veritably transparent; and this transparency had nothing to do with lightness but was rather a manifestation of his weakness. His ability to take up space, to displace air in order to replace it with his body, seemed strangely impaired. Making his way around the city was difficult, and he sensed that it was the hectic commotion of the end of the working day that was propelling him forward step by step, as if he were parasitically feeding on the energy radiating from the people around him, while he himself had no impetus; he didn't know where to turn, and willingly allowed himself to be carried along.

Mathilda hadn't contacted him. He had checked his emails and messages one last time in front of the lift at the hotel. His withdrawal from the conference had been regretfully acknowledged. No word from Mathilda. He had to assume that this development, which had come as rather unexpected for him, was in all respects favourable to her, and she now had free rein to pursue her own plans. She was a very busy woman, and time and time again there had been days on which, overwhelmed by commitments, she was far too busy to have any time for him.

She taught music and mathematics at a high school and trained new teachers. She served as an eminent authority on teaching methodologies, and as a communications wizard and all-round secret weapon; she was, especially when weighed up against his own remuneration, very well paid and highly sought after.

But even in the case of some kind of unanticipated adversity, it must be possible for her to find a free minute to make contact with him. He decided to hold his ground and wait. After everything that had happened it was clearly up to her to make the first move. Quite possibly she hadn't dared approach him now that he knew about her indiscretion and she could be certain of his wrath. Well, the onus was on her to convince him to forgive her. Just the fact that she hadn't got in contact at all was an outrageous affront. He was absolutely not going to run after her, he wasn't going to grovel, he didn't want the humiliation to go so far that he would give in, so to speak, and turn the other cheek. He did regret, however, that under these circumstances she didn't know that he had taken it upon himself to make this journey, Gilbert Silvester, alone in Tokyo, farther from home than he had ever been before. There was no one else he could have told. Mathilda would have delighted in the sight of the Japanese islands from such a high altitude just as much as he had.

The crowds surged toward the underground stations and bus stops. He turned down a side street filled with small bars. It was essentially a ravine densely surrounded by high-rises, and yet oblique beams of evening sun were still managing to reach it. He sat down in a sushi bar at a counter with a view out the window and watched people rushing by. Businessmen, secretaries, schoolchildren, a few housewives. All in all, beardless people. Smooth black hair, smooth faces, smooth rehearsed smiles. A young man sauntered past, he had a full beard and white aikido trousers, his head of hair drawn up into a samurai topknot, but you could tell even from a distance that this beard's wearer was European. There are many theories circulating on the subject of the Japanese beard. The dreariest was biological: some Asiatic peoples are missing a gene or whatever is responsible for beard growth, so that they can only grow patchy beards, if at all, which, in their sparseness, don't function as a status symbol and are preferably shaved off. According to another theory, these beardless men in their prime have simply grown accustomed to fitting in, because companies demand a neat appearance from their employees, which under no circumstances includes beards. Hence, one would never catch a so-called 'salaryman' in Japan fully dedicated to his professional life with even a hint of a beard. The third theory has to do with the overall obsession with cleanliness that the Japanese have. A man on the street with a beard has evidently not conformed to the conventions of bathing that day and is basically unclean: a horror in the land of purism. The crucial question on beard styles and the image of God wasn't related to these theories even remotely. While Gilbert Silvester had so far taken a rather Eurocentric approach to his investigation, a whole new field of research had now opened up to him by being here. This could, he told himself, even give his trip a sense of purpose. He had spent a long time with Michelangelo's depiction of God in the Sistine Chapel. God, carried on a cloud of the finest putti, God, lying there reaching out his hand to Adam with such a casual gesture, and giving him, with the tiniest electrified touch of his completely limp finger, the breath of life; God has a full beard. As Michelangelo famously loved men, the cultural impact of the Sistine Chapel on gay culture was not insignificant for Gilbert's study. Going completely against the narcissism cliché that gay men encountered in the consciousness of the intolerant public, he proposed that the gay man didn't identify with God in the slightest, but rather with the youthful, muscular but nevertheless exceptionally passive Adam. According to Gilbert's reasoning, this Adam, made in the form of the Greek statues of athletes devoid of any body hair, significantly contributed to the present-day fashion for full-body waxing. God, on the other hand, was the one breaking the Freudian touch taboo, the eroticizing force, the wholly other, the great Other, and he hadn't prevented the artist creating him, in the best Renaissance manner, in his own likeness, especially as far as his beard was concerned. Naturally it would be a fruitful undertaking to make a comparative study of this godly beard of the European tradition with a Japanese variety.

The smooth-cheeked Japanese men streamed past the window, and Gilbert suddenly felt comforted. Had he not found a purpose? A reason to be here? He ate his sushi, even though he didn't especially like raw fish, and seaweed even less. But he liked the sticky sushi rice, and he found it reassuring that sushi was a relatively self-explanatory dish. It being his first meal in Japan, he had no interest in taking part in any big experiments and spooning something or other out of an earthenware pot in which unidentified ingredients had been unified into a cloudy soup. He ate the bite-sized pieces of rolled rice without the layer of fish, ate the rice wrapped in seaweed, then ordered some sake and ate a piece of salmon. It was only then that he noticed how hungry he was. He ate everything, leaving only the thumb-sized squid tentacle.

He walked beneath multi-level motorways, admired the jarring electric advertisements and the meticulous cleanliness of the streets. He simultaneously paid close attention not to stray too far from his hotel. He was good at orientating himself and didn't get lost easily, but the city gave him little confidence. The passersby gave off an air of perfection, absolute self-restraint, an antiseptic quality. There were none of those grubby corners where underdone feelings could accumulate, places filled with carelessly tossed rubbish, where one tends to come across unkempt people, places with disconcerting auras that you want to steer clear of.

Here, Gilbert was in the heart of the crowds, but no one came too close to him. At home people gesticulated in the street, took out their bad tempers on others, and even when they didn't say anything, you could sense how the moods of strangers would overlay your own, how it would immediately contaminate a route through the city. Here, on the other hand, the people seemed like they were made of plastic. It made him a little uneasy. He kept going, tried to keep to the rhythm of the other footsteps, but made sure to pay attention to the way he had carved out. Finally, he recognized the train station he had arrived at. Neo-baroque, red brick, with a domed roof over its entrance. He didn't really know what he was doing here twice on the same day. He longed to be back at the hotel, he longed to be gone. Was it homesickness, or wanderlust? He longed to be gone, just as far away as possible. Here he was, however, at the other end of the world, relative to where his home was, and it would hardly bring relief to add a few extra kilometres to the distance he had already covered. He entered the station, a hall of confidentiality that whispered to him all the things he already knew here: the ticket machines, the barriers, and the ticket inspectors, he had seen it all today already. He bought a ticket from the machine and took the escalator up to the platform.

Meanwhile, it had become completely dark. The passengers stepped in and out of cones of light on the platform, the night an impenetrable wall behind them. Gilbert lingered on the platform and watched the trains come in. The Shinkansen pulled in elegantly. The aerodynamically formed locomotive tapered off to a beaky point, giving the train the appearance of a snake-like dragon, a silvery water dragon, iridescent and smooth. Then a train came in that had stunning barbels painted on it, yellow and red, like flames. Gilbert would have liked to have taken notes, but the leather satchel containing his writing things was back at the hotel. Flowing out from behind the next train's headlight, where the outer shell of the bodywork thickened to the upper lip of the dragon, a magenta line ran across all of the carriages, whiskers in the airstream, ancient, endlessly long beard hair, nestled close to the body in flight.

Exhilarated, Gilbert took a step closer to the train, and while the cleaning service stormed through the carriages, collecting rubbish and vacuuming the seats, he dared to give the magenta line a little pat. The passengers climbed on board, the train pulled away, and Gilbert looked after it for a long time. Then he looked for a deserted section of the platform, leaned against a billboard, and called Mathilda.

– Gilbert here, he said formally.

– Where are you?

– I'm in Tokyo.

– What did you say?

– I said: Tokyo.

– That is a very bad joke.

Feeling sorry for herself. Extortion tactics.

– No one's trying to make a joke.

– Why are you tormenting me? What have I done to you?

She actually managed to say it and then wail. Her! She had managed in the space of a few words to go from the role of the culprit to that of the victim. He heard her gulping down the telephone, he thought he could hear tears hitting some surface or other; he hated, as he always had, the irrational female strategy of conducting a conversation while simultaneously not conducting one, or at least abruptly taking it in a completely different direction than the one that could reasonably be expected.

– You haven't tried to call me even once, he said coolly.

– I spent the whole day calling you non-stop. I couldn't get through to you.

– I was on a plane, he said even more coolly.

– But not for over ten hours.

– Like I said, it was a long-haul flight, he said.

He heard her hiss something that sounded a lot like 'Why do you keep lying to me, you vile man,' but he hadn't quite caught it, and didn't want to conjure up accusations for something she hadn't said for the sake of fairness. Before he could ask her to repeat the sentence, she hung up.

He called her back straight away, but she didn't pick up.

On the one hand it was a relief, because the conversation hadn't gone favourably enough for his taste. On the other hand, he began to worry. She seemed confused. She couldn't understand what was happening. She hadn't at any point understood that he was in Tokyo. Where did she think he would be? Did she expect him to have made it to the moon? Where else would he be if not there, where he was? He resented not only having to justify his physical location, but also being forced to prove it. He was standing somewhere on the ground, she couldn't have cared less where exactly. She hadn't asked even once how he was.

He dialled her number again, their shared telephone number, which was now no longer his, entered it wrong, started over, then gave up.

He slowly walked along the platform, away from those waiting to catch a train, went right to the end of the platform where nobody else was. The markings that people lined up behind before boarding ended here, and a fence began that shielded the passengers from the tracks. Gilbert stood in the shadow of a pillar, he found it comforting. He waited like that for a while, nestled closely to the pillar, he waited for the next train, for the next day, waited for the velvety night, which was held back at an unattainable distance by the lights of the train station.

The commuters ebbed away. A young man with a gym bag over his shoulder walked along the platform toward him. He walked past Gilbert without noticing him, walked slowly, as if pulled by an invisible cord, until he reached the farthest end of the platform and put down his bag with excessive care in front of the fence. He plucked the bag into shape and tried to smooth out the creases, which he kept doing without success. Gilbert watched as the bag caved in and was smoothed down again anew. This corresponded exactly with his own situation: he gave endless effort, but this effort was not recognized.

The young man fussed around the bag and then finally seemed to reach a fragile but satisfactory state for the moment. He took a step back to admire his work, and it was only then that Gilbert realized what it was about the man that had irked him. He had a small goatee: trendy, neat. Gilbert Silvester decided to speak to him.

On the face of it, the matter of beards was quite straightforward. God had a full beard, Satan had a goatee. The latter could, iconographically speaking, be seamlessly traced back to the ancient depictions of the goat-bearded, goat-hooved, and goat-tailed Pan, and even today visual media, especially feature films, fall back on the beard when they need to flag up an undeniably morally reprehensible character. And the younger generation, once they hit puberty, naturally liked to flirt with the bad-guy image. Give themselves a mark of toughness in opposition to the rebuke that they're sissies. A younger generation with no prospects can't help but style themselves in a way that suggests that they are a force to be reckoned with.

The young man turned away from his bag and made a move to climb the fence. Before he could swing his leg over, Gilbert walked up to him. The man, startled, slid down from the fence, vaguely straightened up, and bowed deeply and awkwardly many times. Gilbert formulated the politest possible sentence he could muster in English that started with the empty phrase that he didn't want to bother him. No, he wasn't bothering him at all, murmured the young man from below, while bringing his forehead nearer to the ground, he wasn't bothering him in the slightest. What was bothering him (and at this point he apologized profusely), what had stopped him and made him lose his nerve, was this light that the stations had recently been fitted with, blue LED light, which had been attributed with a mood-lifting effect, a positive, friendly light, installed specially for people like him. He had believed, however, that it would be possible to resist it and carry out his resolution. He was sorry. He had failed.

The young man spoke extremely bad English. Gilbert looked indignantly at the jiggling little beard bobbing up and down. Downward-pointing triangles, according to research, enter the human brain as a threat warning. This paltry lint wasn't far enough along to make a clear-cut triangle. Gilbert thought it would be better to hold off on broaching the subject for now.

He finally settled on saying something appreciative: he had watched him, the way he had tenderly handled his bag. He must be very conscientious. He certainly serves the state and society to the best of his abilities. He, Gilbert, wanted to express his thanks in the name of all foreigners, because this country, Japan, was in excellent condition. Clean, odourless, attractive to tourists.

Gilbert had read somewhere that it was beneficial to start a conversation with a suicidal person to distract them from their thoughts. It seemed to work especially well in Japan, where it was simply out of the question for a young man not to reply to an enquiry by an older man, even if he didn't understand a word of it.

The goatee quivered as the young man picked up his bag and followed Gilbert to the exit.

TAKASHIMADAIRA

Yosa Tamagotchi had been poised to throw himself in front of the train because he was afraid he wasn't going to pass his exams. The bag contained a suicide note, carefully calligraphed and dated. He studied petrochemistry, and his marks were good, but maybe not good enough. Fearful of social exclusion, he grew a beard – he knew no company would hire him in this state. If he were to be unsuccessful, he could just say that it was down to the beard, or should luck smile down on him and a firm took him on anyway, there would be nothing more straightforward than shaving it off. But his exam fear grew, paralyzing him to such a degree that he was no longer capable of thinking, let alone committing anything to memory. Therefore, the exams couldn't possibly have gone well. His parents owned a small tea shop, working day and night to enable him to study. He was an only child and on the cusp of deeply disappointing them.

Yosa sipped carefully at a small beer. Gilbert had taken him to the same sushi bar he had been to that afternoon, had bought him something to eat, and tactfully asked him some not too personal questions. They made Yosa squirm like an officer at a tourist office that had been closed for half an hour already, but whose last visitor just wouldn't leave.

He had to get back, he finally said quietly. The last train for the day would be arriving soon.

Nonsense, Gilbert improvised. The station was a bad choice. Unfavourably lit, he had said so himself. Wasn't it conceivable that there was a better place for his intentions?

Yosa Tamagotchi slumped down even further. Of course, he explained, the site wasn't particularly good. There were good and bad places for his purposes. To be more precise, these places in Japan were subject to a strict hierarchy. The cliffs at Nishikigaura Beach on the Pacific Coast were good, the volcanic crater of Mount Mihara was highly suitable, the train stations in Tokyo were bad, they were vulgar, whereas the cliffs, just as an example, transfer their grandeur to those people using them for such an end. He, as a lowly student, had thought the station fitting, but of course he dreamt, as would anyone in his position, of a preordained cliff on the Pacific. This cliff, covered in pine trees, was of a gnawing beauty, and you had to catch the perfect moment when the sun fell on a pinpointed corner of the rocks.

Yosa spoke with great enthusiasm. Then he calmed down and found his way back to the resigned tone of voice that he had evidently reconciled himself to.

We'll find a better place, Gilbert promised grandiosely, and because he said it in an authoritative manner, Yosa nodded compliantly.

They finished their beers, and Gilbert Silvester accommodated the young Japanese man in his hotel room. He had a futon brought up and rolled out against the opposite wall, as far away from his bed as possible. Yosa Tamagotchi, caught out, sussed out, seemed to have come to terms with submitting to Gilbert's additional measures without complaint. The whole evening he had been trembling with anticipation, and now that he was seized by a certain apathy, he felt humiliated and exhausted and fell straight to sleep.

We'll find a better place, Gilbert murmured to himself, but not today. He had missed the chance to call Mathilda again. He didn't want to wake Yosa. He looked at the display anyway. It notified him of forty-three missed calls, but from the previous day, all of them from his wife. She was prone to overdoing it once she set her mind to something. He put on his pyjamas and took the books he had bought at the airport out of his leather satchel. The reading lamp at the head of the bed afforded a sharply defined spotlight while the rest of the room breathed glowering nighttime. Gilbert Silvester read a little of Bashō's travelogue. Then he turned off the lamp and lay unsettled for a long time in the dark.

Matsuo Bashō, the great innovator of the haiku, had travelled in the wild, dangerous north of Japan. He walked 2,400 kilometres in total and conceived of his wanderings – full of hardship, anguish, and perils – as a pilgrimage. For one, they led him to notable places around the country, to its sacred sites and monuments, while he followed his revered predecessors, namely the trail of the poet Saigyō, who had walked this path five hundred years before him, visiting the temples and shrines, admiring nature and composing poems at his various stops.

Saigyō came from an ancient, prosperous family. He served at the imperial court and was set to have a glittering career. He was a masterful horseman and brilliant swordfighter, and he possessed great physical beauty. At a poetry contest he wrote the finest poem, and as his prize he received a valuable weapon and an elegant silk robe. It could have all been so glorious for him – he was still young, supple, and full of promise – but then unexpectedly and abruptly he left Kyoto. The transience of all earthly things tormented him, and courtly vanity repulsed him. He left the revered ruler, left his darling wife and child, without further explanation. He took his vows, left his home, the capital, and underwent a long, solitary trek. He yearned for insight, salvation, and enlightenment. He longed for the moon, for moonlight on cherry blossom.

When Bashō set forth he was forty-five years old, and had five years to live. He was already renowned at this point, and saw himself idolized by students, friends, and patrons, but his fame had become a burden to him. All these people were distracting him, taking him away from poetry.

Like his inspiration, Saigyō, Bashō travelled through the north to leave everything worldly behind him. It required him to turn away from society, just as it had for Saigyō, in order to follow his poetic vision, to cultivate a fresh look at the world, a radical innovation of his poetry.

Bashō sold his hut, his possessions, took leave of his friends, and headed into the pathless heartland. It would be a physical journey as much as a spiritual one. Bashō had a vision. Like Saigyō, centuries before him, he longed for the moon. He longed for the moon over Matsushima.

Matsushima, the most beautiful place in Japan, the bay of pine islands. Gilbert liked that idea immensely. His own situation was similar, after all, he had left everything behind, had abruptly turned his back on everything: got as far away from worldly existence as he possibly could. Just like Saigyō, he had left his wife in the dark about his plans, even cancelled the conference.

The travellers to Matsushima were *lunatics,* moonstruck, eccentric. They composed their own sacred legends; everything was worthless to them apart from poetry, and for them poetry stood for the spirit's path to nothingness. They were extremists, ascetics, mad for a certain kind of beauty, the fleeting beauty of blossom, the ambiguous beauty of moonlight, the hazy beauty of the secluded landscape.

Gilbert imagined the full moon over black pines. A silvery light, diffused over bristly silhouettes, the fuzzy physiognomies of old vagrants. Wandering monks. Artists with knee-length beards. He grinned excitedly into the depths of his room, into the depths of the universe, and boxed his unduly yielding pillow into shape. He had a purpose.

At some point he fumbled around in the complete darkness for his mobile phone and the display lit up blue. Twenty-five thousand missed calls had been received, and he hadn't noticed a single one of them. Maybe there was something wrong with the phone. There was no point listening to the answering machine, he would be occupied for days, nights, to get through this plethora of messages. If someone really wanted something from him they could call again.

Twenty-five thousand phone calls, 25,000 pine needles, shimmering in the moonlight. The pine needles wavered in the wind, then they fell from their branches and formed into field lines, like iron filings drawn by a magnet. A wispily dashed-out sketch, roving hatchings that turned in on themselves. Grey asphalt everywhere, oppressive void. A train platform, a fence. An abundance of eddying pine needles. The train pulled in.

Gilbert Silvester was awoken by sounds coming from the bathroom. The young Japanese man had neatly rolled up the futon and had stowed it away behind the white cube furniture so that it took up practically no space at all. The door to the bathroom ended about ten centimetres above the floor. White steam rolled out from the gap. Against the wall to the bathroom was Yosa's unzipped sports bag. Without touching anything, Gilbert allowed himself a peek inside. Some laundry, paper, and writing materials. On top of everything was a book whose cover showed an amateurish drawing of two coffins and whose Japanese title was – a trendy touch – also printed in English. *The Complete Manual of Suicide*. A typically underground book for a typical clientele, the sophisticated but uptight student with a late-adolescent demeanour and an ill-defined, foolish self-image. Yosa acted reticent but was secretly megalomaniacal. Gilbert's students behaved quite similarly. Precarious existences who already knew that they would always be precarious existences – perhaps this was why they favoured gathering in his seminars: he was a good role model in that respect.

In the hope that Yosa Tamagotchi would be in the bathroom awhile longer, Gilbert called Mathilda.

It took a long time before she picked up. He was already regretting having taken the initiative. In the present situation he had assumed she would indeed be waiting for his call. Yet she sounded displeased.

– It's the middle of the night!

Furious at himself, he suddenly realized that he'd not taken the time difference into account, and apologized.

– Sorry, I didn't take into account the time difference.

– Right, because you're in Tokyo.

She spoke with a sarcastic undertone.

– I admit it's a peculiar feeling finding myself in a different time zone than you.

This was supposed to have been a gesture of reconciliation, if not a declaration of love.

She hesitated a moment.

– And when are you coming back?

He was stunned into silence because he hadn't even asked himself this question.

– As of yesterday evening the situation has become more complicated, he finally said, looking toward the bathroom door, which Mathilda wasn't able to see.

– Then I'll assume you're going to be a while. Maybe you can get back in touch when the situation has been clarified, she said snappily. The conversation was over.

Water had been running for quite some time in the bathroom. Gilbert knocked gently on the door. One couldn't be too careful;

the young man could possibly be preparing, against all of Gilbert's advice, to drown himself in the bath. But Yosa answered without delay that he would be right out.

Gilbert had to send Mathilda a comprehensive text message. Otherwise she might get the idea of going to the police and registering him missing, or as non compos mentis, or both. They'd locate his smart phone and verify the position as Tokyo, thereby confirming Mathilda's assessment. He had always been irritated by her inflexible world view and had found her a bit too much of a neurotic perfectionist. A great number of people fly to New York for a shopping weekend or spontaneously travel to Australia to go surfing – why should he of all people be declared insane for a short trip to Tokyo? He was an adult, legally competent, he'd paid with a credit card, he wasn't accountable to anyone. Saying that, he thought it would be best for now if he told his wife it was a research trip. Pioneering insights into the beards of the Japanese. Mathilda was predisposed to accept without hesitation anything that served the purpose of professional advancement. With this in mind, he began to type a long letter on the minuscule type pad.

While Gilbert was still writing, Yosa vacated the bathroom wearing a white terry-cloth bathrobe, rooted around in his bag, sat down cross-legged in front of one of the all-purpose cubes with a piece of paper, and began writing a new suicide letter. He decorated it with an ink drawing of Mount Fuji, which was hardly recognizable because it was swimming in a cloud of fog. Gilbert sighed. On the one hand, the young man had accepted his authority, was already emulating him (he wrote when the time for writing had been declared), knew how to use the furniture, and was behaving in an overall calm manner.

On the other hand, he was indulging too much in the theatrics of youth. One suicide note after the other, Fuji not clearly defined but rather as if seen through tears. He was soft, and a test of one's patience, mommy issues personified.

They went to the breakfast room together and sat at a table by the window. Yosa ate a bowl of nondescript rice porridge and drank green tea. He had put on a fresh white shirt, and his hair gleamed. Gilbert noticed that he was very slim, sat up very straight, and moved his hands exceptionally elegantly. He himself had assembled a continental breakfast from the buffet. Coffee, toast, scrambled eggs, orange juice. While he ate, he endeavoured not to look at the bowl of porridge. Grey and slimy. It was beyond comprehension that Japan was considered a highly civilized country.

They ate in silence. Yosa waited with his head bowed until Gilbert put down his knife and fork. Then he humbly thanked him for his help, compassion, and accommodation. Gilbert had given him courage. He would forever be indebted to Gilbert, and if he couldn't pay back his debt in this lifetime he should contact his parents, who would be only too glad to give him their finest tea. With both hands, he carefully handed Gilbert a small note bearing an address, bowed deeply, and informed him that today he would be travelling to a better place.

Gilbert raised his eyebrows disbelievingly and immediately saw Yosa give himself away. A tiny sign of doubt on his part, it instantly flew like the shadow of a flock of crows across Yosa's face. Hands in his lap, back straight, and with his head bowed, Yosa explained that he owned a handbook. In this handbook there were descriptions of good, bad, average, and excellent places. He had made his choice and found a place in a much better category.

Gilbert attempted a neutral face.

Wonderful, he said. He'd come along.

On the way to the underground, Yosa carried the gym bag with the handbook inside. Gilbert had his leather satchel and had taken Bashō's travelogues with him. He hadn't got very far with it, but its approach had already won him over. Asceticism, restraint, and humility, a poverty of spirit. His own project of abandonment also entailed making a clean break. A break between himself and society, himself and social conventions, himself and the bizarre pressures of omnipresent turbocapitalism. A pilgrimage in maximum seclusion, in order to find a way back to autonomy, which differed greatly from the kind of freedom that dutiful citizens got out of their money. He himself was not overly wealthy, but it had been enough to take an unexpected long flight. A trip that, as it had already turned out, by no means presented the solution to his problems. A trip that his wife didn't even believe in.

They took the Mita Line to Takashimadaira. Yosa bought them both tickets, steered Gilbert through the subterranean labyrinth of escalators and tiled walkways, and swiped two seats for them on the train. The journey would be long, he explained, they were travelling almost to the final station. He lifted the gym bag onto his knees, took out the handbook, and immersed himself in his reading without another word. Gilbert did the same but was unable to concentrate. He closed his eyes and for a long time listened to the rumble of the carriage, to the sound of the doors opening and closing over and over again. After some time had passed, he woke with a start when Yosa gently tapped him. It was time to get off. Yosa passed him his book, which must have slipped out of his hands. Matsushima, the Japanese man said appreciatively. Ah, Matsushima! he said, clearly moved, and Gilbert watched the goatee tremble pathetically.

They left the station and found themselves once more in a faceless suburb. Yosa followed the directions printed in his handbook. Gilbert trotted along beside him. He felt awfully exhausted all of a sudden.

Prefabricated buildings. All built the same, all ten storeys high. Rundown, squalid. A cut-rate neighbourhood, a deprived area. It looked like Berlin-Hellersdorf. Like the outskirts of Moscow. Like Siberia. If there was a propitious place more suitable than a station in Tokyo in the immediate vicinity, it didn't reveal itself to Gilbert.

Yosa led him through a shopping centre, where a couple of children were skateboarding. No one was shopping. They walked past the housing blocks until Yosa approached one of the front doors. It wasn't locked. A bare entrance area, no parked strollers, no rubbish, only a newly painted white wall that seemed as sterile as a sanitary facility. No cozy abode. The lift was out of service, and they climbed the stairs up to the tenth floor, and from there up onto the roof using the fire ladder. No one stopped them. The whole undertaking was utterly banal.

There was a clear view from the roof, but chiefly of the other rooftops on the estate at an equal height. As if you were standing on a vast, grey expanse disrupted in some places by deep trenches. On the farthest edges of this expanse, far in the distance, the mountains seemed to begin, enveloped in heavy cloud, just like in Yosa's letter. Was one of them Fuji? Gilbert couldn't make it out. He instinctively looked around for an information board, like the ones installed at Swiss vantage points to bring tourists closer to mountain vistas. A panorama that reproduced the contours of the vistas in fine lines, and gave their names and heights.

The roof, however, was empty. Gilbert didn't want to ask Yosa whether his handbook had more detailed information. Naturally a view of Mount Fuji would be an obvious plus point for this location. On the other hand, it could be just as likely that the handbook laid out completely different criteria and had recommended this spot because it featured absolutely nothing of interest. A place so depressing and dismal that it would optimally support a world-weary young man to carry out his resolve.

Yosa for his part didn't seem completely sure whether the quality of the roof met his requirements. He walked around the edge a number of times, looked down onto the street, then came back and assessed the other side. The whole of the front of the apartment block was fitted out with balconies where the residents dried their laundry. A pink hooded sweater fluttered continuously over the railing directly under them, spinning on its drying rack over the drop and then returning to its original position.

Yosa leafed through the handbook again, which apparently had tips for the most suitable direction, because afterward he orientated himself onto the street side of the roof, measured out distances with long strides as if he wanted to take a run up, and checked the slip resistance of the roof with the soles of his shoes. After a phase of estate agent–like activity he was suddenly calm, sat cross-legged on the edge of the roof, and was stilled for a long time in meditation there, his gaze aimed at the point in the distance where Gilbert had assumed Fuji was. Finally he got up, smoothed down his clothes, and indicated that he'd like to entrust Gilbert with his gym bag, bowing all the while. Gilbert didn't take it. He now walked around his side of the roof, kicked out of the way a pebble, which, astonishingly, had made it to these heights, stepped on the edge mounting, which didn't budge. He rattled the fire escape in a workmanlike fashion, and then he had run out of things to do.

Dear Mathilda!

Sublime depth plays an important role in East Asian culture. Profundity, as it's called, is inconspicuous, it's neither this nor that, it's neither loud nor lurid, it is of such a balanced restraint that the less sensitive person, particularly someone from abroad, hardly has the chance to even notice it. It never plays out in the foreground, but it also can't be found in the background, it's far too important for that. Is it something in between, is it prominent? Is it clandestine? It's neither of these things. It is without colour and

flavour, it is without a clear form; it is subtle, it is conceiv-
ably linked with what we also call the sublime in the West.
Only it doesn't reveal itself in power or violence, it isn't
experienced in exorbitance, nor in terms of magnitude or in
being overwhelmed. You won't find it in bold, overhanging,
and, as it were, threatening rocks … etc., but much more in
the quiet contemplation of a dull reed bed or dry autumn
grass, within nature without anything particularly eye-
catching, in a landscape of emptiness and melancholy.
Whether it's a swamp or grass or bamboo that ultimately
forms the contemplative object, turning leaves, a misty
field, or a cloud-topped mountain – what is ultimately
required is a state of mind that allows the sublime to be
seen everywhere. It's believed that this is the cause of the
phenomenon. And, if anything, it possibly comes close to
what is called the Ungrund – the ground without a ground,
the undetermined, the abyss – in German mysticism.

It's too loud here, Gilbert informed Yosa in a dictatorial way.
He could hear the traffic noise, it was absolutely too much to
bear. On top of that, the light was piercing; he had expected
something more subdued, drab surroundings in a pure grey that
absorbed everything around it, so soft that one could barely
perceive oneself anymore. This place, on the other hand, was
full of unpleasant stimuli. It didn't smell very nice, hadn't Yosa
noticed. Urinal deodorizer, window cleaner, washing-up liquid.
Artificial smells, and in far too high a concentration such that,
even to him, as someone who hadn't grown up in this culture,
it seemed un-Japanese, simply not up to scratch.

He went to the fire escape, then he turned – to be on the safe side – to Yosa one last time and explained that this place was absolutely out of the question. Yosa stood there slim and upright on the roof; he wore a thin poplin coat, its tails fluttering, the hanging belt ends dancing at his back like the crepe-paper tails of a kite. He held on to his gym bag very tightly. His face was impenetrable. Gilbert climbed down the fire ladder into the stairwell, his own bag pinned under his arm. He paused, listened. A young couple were fighting behind one of the apartment doors. Someone was playing rock music behind one of the others. He walked down the stairs to the next floor, and then the next one, then the next one. Then he heard the light soles of the young Japanese man's shoes making the iron steps ring out. He waited for him in front of the building. They went back to the underground station without another word.

One could learn from Bashō that all of this had to take place on another level. Consistent long walks. Modest lodgings. Forgoing technical aids, mobile telephones above all. Only then can one distance oneself from the strict superego that seeks to keep everyone under control in everyday life. A state of sovereignty and frugality that will finally allow us to turn toward other things without huge reservations. Inner life. The pines. The moon.

There will be no more of this, Gilbert said sternly when they were once more sitting in his hotel room. He would travel to the pine islands, taking the same route that Bashō took. He would undertake a pilgrimage, a journey of spiritual cleansing, and he, Yosa, would be able to assist him.

Yosa sat on one of the cubes with his head bowed. Gilbert couldn't be certain whether the young Japanese man had properly understood his announcement. He showed no kind of reaction. Maybe he was meditating.

Gilbert lay down on the bed with the Bashō book. After a short while the writing began to swim in front of his eyes. He would have liked to have known what Mathilda was doing at that moment. It was early afternoon, at least it was in Tokyo. He calculated the time difference. Maybe she had just got up. Maybe she was making coffee and setting the table for breakfast. Would she set the table for just herself? Was the long-limbed, ridiculous student teacher already sitting in his place? As soon as he thought of Mathilda, a fireball lifted off from his stomach area, rose to the roof of his skull, and if he blinked even slightly, the whole room was overlaid with his flush of anger. Streaks of blood on the walls, thick drops of it falling from the ceiling, a flickering downpour that had flooded the room up to their ankles. Overcome by wrath, Gilbert stood up, waded over to the second cube, squatted before it, and began to outline the travel itinerary on a hotel notepad. He pressed down hard with the hotel pen. The piece of paper beneath it would be a duplicate for Yosa. They would strictly keep to Bashō's specifications. If the young Japanese man had any special requests, he could let him know.

For dinner Yosa Tamagotchi went downstairs and brought back two bento boxes, which he'd bought from a small shop on the street. In one of the cubes he located a kettle, cups, and tea bags. Gilbert would never have thought of investigating the cubes, but at that moment he discovered on which side the other cube opened. It contained the mini-bar with a range of drinks and snacks.

Yosa brewed some green tea. A pilgrimage characterized by privation, ascetic tea. Gilbert would, inevitably, have to get used to tea.

Yosa opened the plastic box, arranged the chopsticks, poured the tea. Rice with black sesame, carrots cut into flowers, pickled radish, circular cut-outs of tofu, fried whitefish, greyish-green vegetables with small pieces of dyed-pink ginger. After they had consumed their meal in silence, Yosa shyly spoke up. He explained himself.

The estate that they'd sought out that day was one of the most famous in Japan. Social housing from the fifties, a pilot scheme, stable dwellings for people moving out of the countryside into the cities. Electricity and running water, hygiene and modernity. Apartments, though tiny, that would rehabilitate the poorest, the most disadvantaged, the misbegotten of society, create a bell of security, when warm light shone through millions of windows at sunset, when its occupants came home from work to a heated apartment in the winter, they were participating in the achievements of civilization. Naturally the gloss of the place had noticeably faded over the years. Heightened crime rates, neglected buildings. Many stood empty. While other countries boasted about having adopted the principle of simple mass accommodation from the Japanese building tradition, namely from the example of the simple wooden houses with wafer-thin walls and sliding doors, Japan for its part had entered into the Bauhaus movement and considered these new piles of concrete not as a further development of the state-owned architectural style, but far more as a symbol of cosmopolitanism and internationality.

In the meantime, however, it had become a symbol of decline. Those who jumped from these buildings were sending out a message with their deed.

What message, Gilbert wanted to know.

Yosa Tamagotchi couldn't give him an answer.

They went to bed early.

Gilbert dreamt of a gigantic mushroom, as high as a tower block and riddled with holes for windows, as if monstrous snails had eaten through it. It wasn't pleasant living in this mushroom house, because mould was already dripping from the walls and everything was coated in black slime. While still within the dream he felt enraged that the young Japanese man had spread his depressive energy in a manner that had induced corresponding images for him, Gilbert. He couldn't comprehend why the Japanese man couldn't keep his dreams to himself. The boy, he said to himself, sticking his finger contemptuously into the black slime, was really of no use, a total loser.

AOKIGAHARA

Dear Mathilda,

The young man I've taken under my wing in Tokyo will undertake a small trip with me. We are preparing to embark on Bashō's trail, to take a pilgrimage that might make him see sense. Yosa is overly sensitive, completely self-involved, and irreparably spoiled, and thus I proceed on the assumption that it will do him some good to have to tackle long walks on meagre rations and grapple with the beauty of the Japanese countryside, as well as traditional Japanese poetry. Of course, it's absurd that it has to come to this; after all, this is his country, not mine, and I personally – as you may know – have little time, and even less interest, in occupying myself with contemplating plants, waves, and mountain ranges on a foreign continent. However, I see no alternative, I cannot leave the young man in this state. He has wrested an agreement from me that we will visit some locations of his choice while on this journey. Among them are the suicide forest Aokigahara and the Mihara Volcano on the island of Izu Ōshima, where the disillusioned throw themselves into the crater if they want a particularly fashionable end. Unfortunately, these places aren't to be found on Bashō's route, *they're in the opposite direction, in fact, but are still in greater Tokyo, which goes to show that this suicide trend isn't exactly innovative, but instead inhabits known tourist spots. Whatever the case may be, we're starting with his locations for reasons of economy and will then head for the north.*

They left Tokyo by train, then travelled for a while by bus, Gilbert growing more and more annoyed all the while that they were essentially going backward. Instead of north they travelled south, toward Mount Fuji, at whose feet could be found this forest that Yosa wanted to visit at all costs. Yosa carried his belongings in his gym bag, Gilbert only carried his leather satchel. He'd left his suitcase at the hotel – a suitcase was too unwieldly, he wouldn't need a suitcase on a pilgrimage. In his leather satchel he had stuffed his bag of toiletries and some fresh underwear, a fountain pen, ink, a notebook, plus an umbrella and the plastic cutlery from the airplane, just in case. The satchel was a bulky burden on his lap in the bus.

Bashō complained about his excessive baggage on his journey: about the rainproof gear, the weight of his writing and painting utensils, but most of all about the countless farewell gifts from his friends that he hadn't allowed for but could not return and politely had to schlep around with him.

In principle, Gilbert's luggage amounted to what Bashō had packed, minus the paper robe to keep warm at night, because he presumed that they wouldn't be sleeping outdoors, minus the bath kimono, seeing as there wouldn't be an opportunity or time or, as far as he was concerned, even a desire to bathe in public, and minus the leaving presents, as he hadn't received any.

Nor had anyone said goodbye to him. He had left, and no one had shown the slightest interest – what he was doing in this faraway land had been met with indifference. Was there, from a German perspective, any real difference between Tokyo and Tokyo's environs, was there a difference between the main island of the Japanese archipelago and a collection of tiny, scattered islets in an isolated bay on this main island, that's to say, the whole once more in miniature? From a German perspective the journey he was undertaking must seem like one where he wasn't markedly shifting his position; he was both travelling and not travelling. He was travelling a little within a larger journey, which itself, from a German perspective, had been cast into doubt from the outset.

Yosa had given him the window seat, but there was nothing outside to see. From out the corner of his eye he was aware of Yosa beside him devouring heaps of provisions, which he must have bought within a matter of seconds somewhere on the way without Gilbert having noticed. Rice triangles wrapped in seaweed with different fillings that Yosa announced every time he bit into them: salt plum, tuna fish. Some kind of golden mushroom. Beef. Spinach. Hadn't Yosa fully grasped that they were setting off on a journey of hardship and restrictions? Or did he think that this would be his final chance for gluttony? Finally, it all became too absurd for Gilbert, and he allowed himself to be handed a night-black triangle filled with shrimp mayonnaise.

Wilderness. Forests passed by bearing down from a great height, white-grey treetops, luminously swelling clouds that move quickly overhead. Over the multi-lane highway, over the rounded crests of the mountains, the pale mounds floated on higher levels of the air over the endless rice fields, pristine, everlasting, out of bounds, this final natural landscape of water vapour and ice drifted, rough, remote and rugged, bleak and enchanted.

Stratocumulus clouds smeared through the glass of the interurban bus, they continued steadily onward, disseminating unease, longing, an ache to escape to some far-off place.

Gilbert was relieved when they finally disembarked. The bus drove on, and they stood momentarily lost on the edge of the road, the shuddering of the bus still in their bones, dazed by a light vertigo, not quite back to being of this world. Then Yosa sprang into action: he had a plan and a mission, and there was nothing left for Gilbert to do but follow him.

They left the small rest stop that the bus had pulled into and wandered along the main road. They must have been at the foot of Mount Fuji, but the base of Fuji was apparently huge and nothing could be seen of the mountain itself. Gilbert had no conception of whether they had come so close to the mountain that a panoramic view of it was no longer possible because they were already on its slope or whether the mountain was simply concealing its snow-tipped crater in the clouds. Around them was nothing but forest, the sky grey and drab above them, a void of anticipation and uniformity.

Yosa turned off onto a small road, Gilbert went down it after him. For a while he amused himself with the fantasy that they were a miniature caravan, travelling single file through the nothingness. The guide at the front who knew the way, then the camel carrying the luggage. The leather satchel pulled down on Gilbert's arm, so he pinned it under one arm and then the other. The advantages of a nylon backpack. Beyond a certain level of exertion, aesthetic concerns would fade into the background. But they weren't quite at that point yet. Gilbert walked grimly determined at Yosa's back and tried to feel some excitement for this journey. An unremarkable road, leading to a forest car park. The car park was quite big for one that was in the middle of nowhere, and it was surprisingly full. Abandoned cars that hadn't been moved in a long time rotting away, covered with layers of leaves that had collected on the windshield wipers, the hubcaps thoroughly coated in moss, and inside on the seats were crushed water bottles, as if they'd just been finished and discarded, and unfolded maps.

The owners had got out here and not come back, Yosa said in a travel guide's voice, one could say in a know-it-all tone, as if he had personally brought about these conditions and as if it were associated with some heroic achievement that escaped the average person like Gilbert, as if it had to escape them because the average person like Gilbert didn't recognize the higher meaning of disposing of one's car in some wild place and disposing of one's own body shortly afterward, that is, to simply use the world as a waste disposal unit for the spiritual and physical waste one had produced throughout one's lifetime.

Gilbert entered the forest vexed, and while vexed he acknowledged that they were following the papery authority of the suicide handbook, which was leading them down a dull footpath, and then astray.

The forest opened its black wings, closed in around them, drew itself closer and closer together with a sigh. Who is one fleeing when entering this forest? A great leafy being wrapped them in its humidity, wrapped them in its formidable rustling, within its breezing and whispering, its ominous mouldy odour.

They disregarded multiple warning signs. Yosa planted himself next to the first one and translated its advice, so that Gilbert would in no way misunderstand what they would be flouting henceforth: under no circumstances leave the marked routes, otherwise you won't be able to find your way out of the forest. If you are harbouring specific intentions in this regard, you are reminded to think about everything your parents have done for you. Parents shouldn't be disappointed, after all. The rest of society also had a right to the labour of young people, so anyone desperate enough to have reached this point – the warning sign – should call a telephone hotline.

Hanging across the path that turned off from the main footpath next to the sign was a thin cord, which was clearly intended to symbolize a barrier. Yosa raised the symbol, leaned forward, and ducked underneath it, and Gilbert did the same, instantly filled with hot defiance against an official admonition comprised of slack string. They really hadn't needed to accost him with this silliness, treat him like a child with this barrier of packing string; he adhered to a sufficient number of regulations already, albeit reluctantly, and while walking in the forest he didn't need to be monitored or infantilized. He caught up with

Yosa and stomped angrily along the track through the unwieldy, forbidden territory.

Essentially, it was a regular forest. Certainly, the forest was dense and overgrown, the ground was uneven and riddled with knobbly roots. Gilbert swung his bag to the beat of a march. Certainly someone could have got lost here, certainly one could quickly become disoriented because everything looked the same, tree trunks covered in moss, branches, and leafage – a forest like any other, perhaps a drop more humid, a tad darker, a little eerier than the forests Gilbert was accustomed to. But not being able to find one's way out of a forest in a civilized, densely populated country, one that you explore by foot – that required a very special kind of ineptitude.

Gilbert, propelled by a peculiar anger, wouldn't slow his tempo until the path became smaller and smaller and finally completely trailed off between two toppled tree trunks. He sat down on the rotten wood and asked Yosa, who was panting for breath, to give him the handbook.

The handbook showed a site plan with shelters, natural monuments, and vantage points. According to this plan, they had ended up in a somewhat badly explored part of the forest, and the next shelter was quite a long way away. Apparently they had already reached their destination. Gilbert felt no desire to have Yosa explain the Japanese text, and so he relied on the drawings. He turned back a page.

Hanging errors. A too-thin rope that can't sustain your weight and then breaks. Too short a drop. Unstable base for the rope. Incorrect knots. Ridiculous stick people with nooses around their necks sat puzzled on the ground next to a stair rail or a heating pipe or a just-broken branch. A handbook for complete morons, a handbook for people who really hadn't succeeded in life.

He became more and more impatient and wanted to know what was going to happen now. Yosa apologized. The gym bag was too heavy. Couldn't go as fast as him. Didn't have Gilbert's excellent physique. Had to pay attention to where they were going. Follow the instructions. Find the right place.

Behind the rotten trunks, the invisible authority had once more affixed its symbolic restraints. Cords and colourful plastic tape fluttered in all directions, as if the legally traversable forest had now come irrevocably to an end.

Yosa looked all around him, then he got down to it. He fished out a roll of yellow hazard tape and tied it around the end of the rotten tree trunk. He struggled, drew it together, looped and tied it, while Gilbert watched him skeptically. Yosa could at least tie a standard knot, or was he just winding the tape loosely around a couple of times? Far be it for him to interfere; young people have to learn by making mistakes. Once Yosa had set off, he checked the tape with a quick tug; it held.

They broke through the impervious undergrowth, stumbled over roots, fell into holes filled with leaves. Time and time again Yosa had to lift a piece of tape blocking their way, as if someone had frenziedly criss-crossed the whole area in wild zigzags of tape. Yosa for his part gradually uncoiled the yellow tape he had brought and led it with special care over and around obstacles.

This is so, he explained to Gilbert, you can find the way back. Without a guiding line you would get hopelessly lost, roam through the forest for days until you collapsed from exhaustion. Undecided people safeguard their route with this method of marking. Those resigned to their fate use it to mark the place where their remains can be found. The most determined forgo the rope. The yellow tape was for him, Gilbert; he would be able to go hand over hand along the tape and find his way back out of the forest. The handbook recommended yellow because it remained visible the longest when night fell.

He asked Gilbert to carry his gym bag so he could lay out the tape better. Gilbert took the bag in one hand and the leather satchel in the other, found the even distribution of weight pleasant, found the idea of the plastic tape sensible when compared with the bread crumbs and pebbles employed in the pertinent German literature, found himself prepared to concede that the Japanese man had internalized the idea of Ariadne's thread, ancient ingenuity, even if it meant littering the forest with copious waste plastic left behind through the irresponsible indifference of teenage deadbeats, a forest that now seemed unusually beautiful and dignified, very quiet, slightly misty, and of this exceedingly beguiling green that the centuries-old volcanic rock yielded.

Gilbert became engrossed in the diverse green tones while stumbling over branches and bracken with both bags. Supermarket green. The subtle green of a lettuce, the glossy green of a polished apple, bitter spinach green, tender fennel green. Zingy toothpaste green, conservative samani green. With leaves swaying before his eyes, he wanted to exercise a more refined distinction process, revel in the nuances, appoint distinct tones from the memory of the watercolours in his school paint box, bilious green, malachite green, yellowish green, French green, while the wind mingled and parted the trees, making the colours fleeting and indefinable.

Yosa pointed out a pair of shoes filled with leaves, waiting neatly paired together on a moss cushion. A cut rope was swinging from the tree above.

Once a year, day workers comb through the forest and collect the bodies, Yosa explained, and Gilbert couldn't tell whether he had got this information from his handbook or whether he had already known it. And why couldn't the day workers take the discarded rubbish with them too?

Gilbert looked up and remained, even when he tripped, enthralled in the contemplation of the trees. He found himself enclosed within the colour of the unspectacular, the normal, the proper. In Japan, the flora brought him a strange sense of relief. One was always surrounded by unproblematic azalea green, positive moss green, humble bamboo green – and the mystical dark green of the pines. They stand massive and bursting with bright needles, and he ducked into their shadow, into their cicada green, their sea green, their airstream black. The bulky, sky-blotting canopy shifted before his eyes while he crossed the rough forest floor, cut-outs of dark needles, cut-outs in which something lavish mops the white sky, unrecognizable in its detail, ungraspable in its uniqueness, no firm image. He walked over the uneven ground, he walked beneath the evergreen pines, their verve, their darkness and richness of detail, he walked in the splendour of their gazillion needles, and the closer he tried to look at them, all the more the tree withdrew, disappeared in his attempt to find a language for it. Gilbert felt inclined to devote himself to the pines at length, to the fragments of pines and pines in their entirety, with the possibility or impossibility of their existence. He was looking forward to travelling to the pine islands.

He drew Yosa's attention to the pines, but Yosa shook his head. The Japanese red pine, akamatsu, with which this forest was mostly populated, is considered female, Yosa explained, while the Japanese black pine, omatsu, which is chiefly found on the coast and so grows on the islands, is perceived as being male. This was a popular subject of classical literature, two ancient pines, man and woman, growing far from one another, united in spirit. It effortlessly illustrates the various levels of dreamlike reality.

So, it's a forest of female red pines. A forest as if specially made for people with mommy issues, dark, devouring. The ideal forest for suicidal people who secretly wish to once more fuse with the all-powerful, devastating, dismissive object of their earliest childhood. The suicidal person turns away from the material plane occupied by the body to the spiritual plane merely in order to force the maternally conceived object to understand, to wrest from the object the affection and attention denied them their whole life. The suicidal person gives themselves up, they sacrifice themselves, but it is a treacherous sacrifice, solely for the purpose of softening the object's indifference, a sacrifice only in appearance then, whose aim is loving devotion through a form of severe evasion. Yosa was mistaken, however, if he believed he would achieve his goal with such a course of action. Maybe his relatives would shed a tear, light an incense stick, inform their wider relations, but to achieve anything more than this shallow effect would be too much of an effort. Because ultimately this wasn't a suicide from one's own free will, from a serene mindset, ultimately it wasn't an independent decision, but a pitiful attempt at manipulation. Juvenile behaviour that made one ridiculous in death. One only had to look at the disgusting, half-decayed figures that unfortunately abounded in this forest. If one's intention was that at least death would give a lost life dignity in retrospect, then this method beneath the red pines was in any case doomed to fail. Gilbert thought his own project of abandonment was preferable. Black pines on a cliff, solitary, autarchic, and sprayed by salty surf. He kept his opinion to himself, but he couldn't condone this young Japanese man exposing himself in such a manner.

They found a fully dressed skeleton in the moss, they found dried bouquets of flowers on a tree stump, whose bearers had apparently followed one of the tapes, they found single pages of the handbook bearing the map that had become wavy from the moisture, they found a lady's handbag containing a solemn suicide letter written on a wooden tablet, they found more ropes dangling from the trees, their cut nooses lying on the ground. Gilbert presumed that he was carrying a similar rope through the forest in the gym bag, perhaps even two.

They had made incredibly slow progress. When the safety tape had been completely unrolled, the sun was already going down. Dusk came early in Japan: one got up early, ate lunch before twelve, ate dinner in the afternoon, and when it got dark around seven, the day was declared over. Gilbert decided to do precisely that.

He sat down in the leaves and praised Yosa for the perfect planning and execution of their excursion. Yosa reluctantly sat down next to him and claimed back his bag. Gilbert passed the bag over, he couldn't feel what it contained. Yosa rummaged inside and brought out two flasks of green tea. One for Gilbert, one for him.

Gilbert renewed and intensified his praise, Yosa shook his head repeatedly. The tea, cold and sticky, wasn't quite sweetened to the point where the tea could no longer be tasted. A sugary liquid whose tea-like qualities prevailed, slightly bitter, slightly grassy, a mild tea green in tone that could no longer be discerned by the time Gilbert had emptied half the flask. The colours all disappeared, the forest suddenly changed from green into grey tones, then it was completely dark.

Gilbert, Yosa suggested, might now set off on the return trip. The excursion had ended here, the provisions spent, and if he left now, keeping to the tape, he'd still make the bus to Kōfu. Yosa knelt before him and bowed his forehead several times to the ground.

No, Gilbert said. He stood up in order to make his voice more powerful, and it suited him that Yosa stayed cowering on the ground because it only strengthened his position.

He couldn't get his head around Yosa not having the power of judgment. Barely any decency, hardly any sense of pride, and no taste whatsoever. The place was untenable, it was a dump, it didn't allow one to really experience nature, and above all it was too full, an often-frequented forest completely overcrowded with suicides, a mass grave. Yosa had to think better of himself than that. The handbook was no good, it only pointed to general places that anyone could know, it misled people because it withheld the real places.

He couldn't make out Yosa's reaction in the dark. He kept speaking in the same vein for a few more minutes, until the forest floor began to whimper.

We're going back, Gilbert ordered, we're going back and taking the bus to Kōfu. And he expressed his hope that Yosa would be able to find them accommodation there.

Yosa passed him the gym bag in silence and felt for the loose end of the safety tape. He asked Gilbert to stay close to his heels, then felt along the tape and carefully began to roll it back up. After a few metres Gilbert had already been left behind. The forest shielded the luminous night; it was so dark that he could barely proceed on the uneven ground, especially with their bags. Yosa took the rope out of his bag and tied the two of them together. Gilbert felt the knot in front of his stomach. Was Yosa really capable of tying a noose? Had he made do with a simple overhand knot? The gym bag at his elbow, Gilbert fingered the knot's contours and came to the conclusion that Yosa had tied an obi knot, like the one people use for judo belts, and must have put the noose around his own waist. Why hadn't the young man thought to bring a torch, candles, matches, anything? Why? Because we've come to know the boundaries of his abilities, his shortsighted planning, his inefficient actions. For a while they proceeded in centimetres. Yosa meticulously rolled up the once-yellow tape, bit by bit, so that it didn't break. Gilbert let himself be pulled along by the waist; he leaned back and made it heavier so that Yosa would indirectly get a sense of the weight of the bags. Then they came to a point when multiple tapes crossed one another.

Their own tape had unfortunately become twisted and tangled with the others, Yosa had led the tape so clumsily through the bottleneck that they could no longer tell which one was the tape that had led them here. Could they distinguish a variation in the breadth, thickness, material? Could one decipher the colour yellow through an acute enough sense of touch? Gilbert hadn't taken the forest seriously up to this point. He hadn't taken the guiding line seriously, not even the noose. Now it looked like they would have to wait out the sunrise in this particular corner of the forest where an especially large amount of plastic had built up.

Night in the forest. It was still early evening, the night would be long. There was a cracking sound, a rustling, something moved incessantly, the forest shifted nervously all around them. Gilbert held on tightly to the leaves, to the moss; he smoothed down the ground, threw small hard twigs to the side, leaned back his head on the gym bag, and put the leather bag on his lap. That's how he would stick it out till morning. He couldn't see exactly how Yosa was lying. He had most likely got silently down on his knees and was now bathing in his limitless failings. The rope hung slackly between them, still binding them to one another. In case he got the better of Gilbert while he slept, the youngster couldn't just disappear.

But Yosa made no move to do anything. The forest swished and gasped, and Yosa shuffled closer to Gilbert. Trembling, he awaited the ghosts.

Every suicide, he blurted out, would become a vengeful spirit and seek out the living to drag them into death. It was bad news to spend the night in a forest seething with wrathful spirits. He could hear them whispering already, he could hear their voices everywhere, they sounded like dry autumn leaves and spoke at him endlessly.

Gilbert agreed with him. That's the way it is when you're dead, he said maliciously. Total darkness and non-stop claptrap.

Then he reconsidered and changed the subject. He wanted to make Yosa think about something else, but he also wanted to talk about something that would interest him too. Traditional beard styles in Japan. What did Yosa know about that?

Yosa didn't make a sound. He was seemingly trying to not even breathe. Could it be that he didn't have the faintest idea about absolutely anything? To give him some encouragement, Gilbert gave a talk on the subject of the impeccable shaving tradition of the samurai. In the Roman Empire too, he continued, a smooth face was a mark of a sophisticated civilization, whereas the uncouth forces outside the empire's borders, aptly referred to as barbarians by the Romans, boasted strong beard growth and flowing manes. The irony being that the barbarians on their part regarded their wild hair as a symbol of power, so that ultimately one reaches a stalemate in an assessment of the phenomenon. To this day, the Roman Pope has always presented himself as clean-shaven, while the Russian Orthodox Patriarch of course wears a godlike full beard as a sign of his gravitas, which in turn fosters the thought that the Roman Catholic Church in its combination of the Roman and the Catholic poses within itself a contradiction, since God's representative on earth apparently didn't trust himself with the divine look, but rather studiously cultivated the facial component of the Adam costume. An occasion for pedantic theoretical discussions and a consequential application of Kantorowicz's 'the King's two bodies' theory, according to which the ruler by the grace of God fell into two corporeal categories, the body natural of his private person and the divine body politic ex officio. The insignia of the papacy, the shepherd's crook, the Ring of the Fisherman, etc., testified to a wholly immaterial power whose realization the physical papal body didn't have even the slightest stake in, so that whatever kind of beard growth was under discussion, it had to rightly be construed as an intolerable presumption and arrogance, namely as a confusion of the divine and the earthly. Where the Orthodox Church stood in all this, Gilbert wanted to work out more precisely; it was in any case, he explained to Yosa, of the highest interest for his project.

In Japan, on the other hand, the dichotomy of clean and dirty predominated. The samurai, as an agent of the state, and therefore also a representative of high culture, had to be of the utmost purity, whereas for the wandering wise man who had turned his back on the world, that is, the city and its mannered pleasures, it was not only permitted but downright fitting for them to cultivate the philosophical beard that a life connected with nature, a life by the simplest means in the solitude of the mountains, a life of wandering equipped only with the bare necessities, demanded.

With this night in the forest, Gilbert solemnly declared, their pilgrimage had begun fairly authentically – and in accordance with this fact he himself would now also keep his beard. Yosa, with his antagonistic goatee, had of course already taken a step in that direction; he, Gilbert, would accompany him in every respect.

Gilbert adjusted the gym bag, lay down in a more comfortable position and, momentarily overcome by his own solemnity, closed his eyes. Then he once more heard the crackle of the forest, he heard the rustling getting louder and coming closer. He heard the young Japanese man sobbing uncontrollably.

Yosa Tamagotchi, son of a tea trader, wore a false beard. Restrained and dutiful by nature, he had been teased for being a girl since he was a child. He drank mostly tea, hardly ever cold beverages, almost never alcohol. He was invested in body care, in bath essences and perfume, in nice clothes. This is where he acted out his sense for aesthetics: he liked going shopping. A derisive label for these young types had been around for some time in Japan: they called people like him the 'herbivore men' or 'grass-eater men.' For people like him, sets of artificial beards were available, somewhat sparser so that they would seem all the more real, beards in slightly unseemly shapes, which would give their wearer that certain something, a whiff of nonchalance, even recklessness, qualities that his upbringing hadn't provided him with and which he couldn't see himself developing. His only friend studied at a different university, they had lost touch. He had never had a girlfriend. His father despaired because he hadn't taken over the tea business. His mother had withdrawn her support and empathy for the same reason. He was interested in soft skin and after finishing his studies in petrochemistry he wanted to develop skin creams with seaweed extract. His parents found this unacceptable. The artificial beard could stay affixed for only a few days. While they were hiking in the forest the current model had fallen off his chin without him noticing. There were further specimens in Yosa's gym bag. Gilbert ought to take care not to put excessive pressure on the bag.

At some point the snivelling eased off. The forest still shuddered sometimes, then Yosa's breathing quieted down, and Gilbert could hear that he had fallen asleep. Alone in the dark, there was nothing left for him to do but wait for the ghosts. He fancied that it was getting easier to make things out, that his eyes had become accustomed to the equalizing greyification, that when he looked up he could discern the anthracite grey foliage standing out against the night-grey sky.

The last time Gilbert had been in a forest – it had been a very long time ago – it was with Mathilda. He hadn't considered himself a forest-lover. At first Mathilda had made him take trips into the woods with her, and he couldn't say that he had enjoyed it. It was during his time as a visiting professor in the US, which had led to nothing in terms of his career progression. He would have been better off staying exactly where he was and winning a post in Germany, but in the conviction that it could be beneficial for his career he went to an insignificant university for two semesters in the provinces, and his career plateaued as he taught poorly attended German courses in which he would confront his students with a cultural theory text every once in a while.

He spent most of his time at his desk in the small rented timber house, he looked out over cultivated lawns and majestic trees, awaiting autumn.

In October, Mathilda came to visit for two weeks. Soon the leaves began to change colour. It was only in a few parts of the world, they say, that it is as spectacular as it is in North America, in the region of the Great Lakes. It can be observed in only a few places in the world because a large part of the world's surface consists of evergreen plants, tropical rainforests, or conifers. Central Europe, as in Canada, as in New England, has large areas of deciduous forest, but in Central Europe the turning of the leaves doesn't create that much of a fuss, it's regarded as a matter of course, a natural phenomenon that one takes as much for granted as the weather. Maybe someone poeticizes the season or the flash of colour every once in a while, *The beech forest flushes autumnally, like a patient inclining toward death; The leaves are falling, falling as though from far away, as if distant gardens were withering in the sky*; but these are singular examples of poetic eccentricity.

In North America, on the other hand, the turning of the leaves provokes a hysterical euphoria that compels people out of their homes and into the woods. The cause is the sugar maple that grows particularly extensively at this latitude, from which bronze maple syrup is harvested and whose foliage in certain weather conditions displays a scarlet red, madder red, pontifical red. The miracle lasts a couple of days, and then the leaves turn brown, wither, and fall from the branches. Prior to this, though, they run through the entire spectrum from dark green to light green, yellow and orange to fire red and deep red, and this spectacle of colour blazes through the entire country, heading down from the north. Throughout the autumn months, foliage-spotters give updates on the state of various spots, announcing the beginning, the flux with its coloured gradients, the peak, the dazzling red, and its abeyance so that interested nature-lovers have the opportunity to betake themselves to each of these places for the great erubescence.

Mathilda came to visit so that she could be closer to him, but she also came to see the turning of the leaves.

Not from his desk, nor from the lavish gardens surrounding his wooden house, not anywhere in the spacious estate (which, in German terms, would be categorized as a park) was a sign of the colouration to be found. In the Foliage Reports that started on Labour Day on the first Monday of September and were updated every three days, the map of the northeast states was resplendent in a seamless green. But Mathilda was burning to see the red maple forests, and she was determined to travel long distances; therefore, as far as Gilbert's professional obligations allowed, they indeed travelled extensively on this most expansive of continents.

The turning of the leaves facilitates pure presence; up to a certain degree it is unforeseeable, it is difficult to plan for, and it certainly can't be done far in advance. Those who desire to see the red autumn leaves must cast off everything, must leave everything behind, and go.

They drove with a rental car to Maine and Vermont, they drove along the Kancamagus Highway through the White Mountains of New Hampshire, they drove to Canada. Gilbert had found these trips in remote forests ridiculous. After hours in the car driving down the same expressways and rural high-ways, after hours of mediocrely coloured trees endlessly gliding by on both sides of the car, still green at the bottom, going reddish at the tips, absolutely unspectacular and no different to the ones found along the autobahn in Spessart, after many monotonous hours they would get out somewhere at a recom-mended place, enter the forest, and the trees would be even harder to make out than they were before.

They often fought on these road trips. The temperature remained above average, the leaves didn't change colour. It was only after Mathilda had already left that the first autumnal cold period set in, the foliage flamed up, his house was surrounded by tremendous flares, and the crimson splendour crushed him because it had come too late. It was too late, it couldn't be fixed, and he was alone.

Dear Mathilda,

    An itinerarium is a travel guide that presents the most common paths and roads, information regarding lodgings, costs, and transport, and also offers up the experiences of those who have already tackled this very same route.

    Bashō's travelogue bears the title Oku no Hosomichi; oku is usually translated as hinterland, backroads, interior, deep north, etc., but the geographical significance of the province or heartlands aside, oku can also be read as human interior and means less the body and its innards and far more the inner landscape of the human consciousness. There-fore, Bashō's travels can also be read as a mental excursion, and they can be read as an adventure of the spirit.

In the West, Saint Bonaventure undertook a spiritual journey not dissimilar in character to Bashō's travels in the East. In his Itinerarium Mentis in Deum he describes the mind's road to God, whereby it should be noted that it is less a travelogue and more a manifesto for contemplation. Just like in Zen Buddhism, a didactically motivated meditation practice is exercised that has the goal of not only promoting serenity and well-being, but also of leading the adept to enlightenment – Bonaventure's method also culminates in the mystical union – and the complete spiritual disenfranchisement and discouragement of Christian laypeople through a pyramidically structured church is presumably attributed to there not being such a systematic approach that guarantees divine vision in our cultural sphere.

What I'm driving at is that our inward journey is taboo, that this interior is not only a divine space and therefore looking inward is regarded as an imposition, but that it is actually difficult to locate. When Bashō contemplated a pine, what was so inward about it? someone might rightly ask, and I ask myself too how someone could read the writings of Bashō, which are so explicitly to do with nature, places of note, and tribulations on a tangible walk, that is, purely with the outside world, as a literature of the inner world? If the outside world is to be placed on equal footing with the space of consciousness, then the distinction between inside and outside is pointless. But it's precisely this, I suspect, that is Bashō's approach, and it is precisely this that made him so famous. Bonaventure *found God in things and through things, Bashō conversely finds things in and through God.*

And we – seeing as we don't understand this inner world – cannot know whether a difference may ultimately lie in the opposite approach or not.

He awoke from a jolt that went through his entire body. It was already light. Yosa had wanted to slink away to answer the call of nature, found that the rope wasn't long enough, and had attempted to climb out of the noose inconspicuously, but had toppled over in the process and had achieved precisely that which he had wanted to avoid, namely, attracting Gilbert's attention. Gilbert raised himself from the moss, stowed the rope away in the gym bag, and began to untangle the safety line that, insofar as theirs was concerned, had recovered its yellowness and now advantageously contrasted with lengths of blue, green, and yellow-and-black plastic tape.

Without further ado, they followed the tape until they found the beaten track, soon reaching the official path, the car park, the bus stop. It wasn't long until the bus came. They stood clearly visible at the edge of the road. The bus didn't reduce its speed and drove past.

Yosa sighed. It's the same bus driver as yesterday, he asserted. He recognized us. He mistook us for ghosts. No one comes back from this forest.

They spent three hours at the bus shelter. The next bus stopped and brought them to the train station, where they took the train to Tokyo.

SENJU

Gilbert dreamt that he was once again, yet again, still, sitting on a train. They were travelling past Fuji, travelling for hours without the mountain getting any closer, without the landscape altering. They were going fast, indeed he could hear the sound of a speeding train, but at the same time they stayed permanently fixed in the same place, here, beleaguered by an impermeable grey that pressed against the window.

Theoretically, they had already travelled past Fuji the day before, past the sacred mountain, the emblem of Japan. When taking the Tōkaidō Line south from Tokyo, one was afforded – weather permitting – a view of Fuji. The train company even used an image of a Shinkansen in front of the slumbering volcano beneath a red evening sun in its promotional material; it had panorama carriages available where one could sit on a swivel chair in front of a very large window. On the outward journey, Gilbert hadn't thought of taking a look at the mountain, as he had been of the opinion that they were headed for this mountain anyway. But the mountain could not be seen from the Aokigahara forest because the trees obscured everything. Now that it had started to rain lightly, the landscape lay beneath clouds and mist, but Gilbert could see a few mountainsides breaking through, their peaks hidden in the fog – was one of them Fuji? If it was, he wasn't able to differentiate it from the other forested foothills of the mountains, and it would only show itself to those who knew it, who were able to determine it by its degree of inclination and who were not dependent on the snowy, fondant icing peak, on the characteristic crater, on the majestic splendour of its full form.

Yosa huddled in his seat and slept, his arms wrapped tightly around his gym bag. This would have been the perfect moment for him to make himself useful, point out Fuji, give a talk about it, read out loud from his book, act as tour guide, but he was just a hopeless case.

When the conductor came, Gilbert inquired as to at what section of the journey Fuji would appear. The conductor was able to readily provide highly detailed information. He nodded and specified a time, gave the exact minute they would pass Fuji. Then he hesitated and gave the subsequent minute instead to allow room to manoeuvre, apologizing profusely that the service was already running with a thirty-second delay, but adding that they might still make up the time.

Gilbert stubbornly pursued the second hand of his watch, pressed himself against the window ten minutes before the given time, stared at the drizzle and at the droplets running down the window pane, and even though he was sure that he could 100 per cent rely on a designated time in strictly regulated Japan, he didn't want to rule out the possibility that his watch was running fast or slow, so he stared into the rain as a precaution, for almost twenty minutes he stared intently through the haze, but there was nothing outside that he could focus on, and Fuji was nowhere to be seen.

Learning to die. The journey that serves to distance oneself from everything, in order to get closer to something, was nothing more than a contemplation of the space that resulted from the journey itself. A move that followed the expansion of the mind, in the space between 'here' and 'there,' while the mind itself, one truly hopes, would find peace; thoughts put themselves in order, the whirlwind of things slows down a little, finding its way back to a long-forgotten form, a place in which the vague and unknown, that which is constantly changing, can be observed. One follows the subtle shifts, the illusory imagery, one really hopes to become clearer about one's own self, that most elusive of things.

Gilbert regarded the tranquil face of the sleeping Japanese man, whose cheek was pressed against the gym bag, and suddenly felt immensely disappointed. Fuji was out of eyeshot, the Japanese man expressed not the slightest, but really, not even the slightest emotion that he could discern, and on the excursion into the suicide forest there had also been as good as nothing to see, since he couldn't in any good conscience describe the rotting clothes of the dead and a few loose bones as 'must-sees.' He felt the disappointment rise from the centre of his chest and enclose his skull in a glutinous fog that arrested all of his mental activity.

When he awoke he found himself back in his hotel room with the white cubes. They had arrived early that evening, had lain down straight away, and lost consciousness. Gilbert still felt dazed. Every movement was difficult, and all his joints ached, as if he had lain on a mound of crooked branches. Yosa was making noise in the bathroom, white steam rising from underneath the door.

Dear Mathilda!

The suicide forest Aokigahara proved to be a flop and we immediately returned to Tokyo. It has confirmed that the young Japanese man's fancies are unrealistic, and I do not want to waste any more time on his shambolic projects. Thus we're commencing the Bashō trip without further delay. Bashō broke free of the then Edo – modern-day Tokyo – with his sights set on the shrouded Fuji and the cherry blossoms of Ueno. After the first leg of the journey he spent the night in a place called Senju, the first post station on the Northland road. Bashō named the starting point of his journey 'The Crossroads of Illusions' in his travelogue. We can get to both Ueno and Senju from our hotel in no time at all on the underground, it would cost us only the morning. Yosa suggested that, seeing as I'll be in Tokyo only once, we could visit the gardens of the old Imperial Palace, which I'm reluctant to do because I didn't make this long journey to Japan only to see my progress hindered by the pleasure-seeking masses at beloved tourist spots. However, Yosa is obsessed with this idea all of a sudden and has been going on and on about how these Imperial Gardens would be the ideal preamble for our actual destination, the pine islands of Matsushima, because they contain a large stand of imperial black pines. So as not to put him in a foul mood, indeed, essentially to motivate him, I have succumbed. Nevertheless, after the

experience in the forest, I don't have any great expecta-
tions regarding the imperial pines and I also no longer
place any faith in Yosa's suggestions; the whole lot has
proved how an undisciplined mind allows itself to be over-
whelmed by muddled feelings and drifts toward irrational
and meaningless acts. I had expected more from a Japan-
ese man. And so it's left up to me to keep my composure,
without making my misgivings apparent in the slightest, to
accompany him to these pine gardens in accordance with
the Zen device: action without action.

As the door to the bathroom swung open, a white cloud swelled up out of it. Only gradually did the outline of a narrow figure in a white bathrobe appear, an apparition in the unknown place between white and white. Gilbert held his breath. The boy appeared translucent, fluid, whittled down. Gilbert was overcome by a faint fear; he didn't dare speak to him, as if Yosa could simply evaporate if addressed too fiercely. The boy, still visibly exhausted, walked over to his gym bag and rummaged around for a fresh false beard.

Before freshening up himself, Gilbert sent Yosa out into the world on a little errand. He asked Yosa to buy him the socks that were atrociously cheap in every supermarket, thin ones, socks that wore out in the blink of an eye, a disposable product in Japan. It wouldn't do any harm to have some new socks on him, even if he didn't necessarily think he needed any. And he wanted to be alone for a while. He found it unpleasant to use the bathroom while Yosa was in the room. He was able to move only with the most extreme caution when going about his washing routine and made efforts to avoid making any noise whatsoever since it became apparent to him that the Japanese boy reacted with great sensitivity to it afterward. The toilet apparatus didn't only offer warm flushing water and a heated toilet seat, it also functioned as a stereo with a wide selection of soundscapes including the sea, rain showers, waterfalls of various heights, and babbling brooks, but also tweeting birds, the wind in desolate treetops, coastal storms, as well as all of Mozart's violin concertos. The mania with cleanliness in this country had gone so far that they even wanted to flush away filthy noises with water sounds. Yosa would put the highest waterfall on while performing his ablutions, so that Gilbert could in fact never tell whether he was showering or brushing his teeth, but since figuring out the point of this device he himself had become self-conscious. Must one really draw attention to their undertakings in the bathroom by placing a layer of noise underneath it? Didn't the intensified water noises only drastically heighten the feelings of shame? Didn't it force people to listen to what else was going on when usually no one pays any attention whatsoever to such things? Gilbert for his part refused to play a background sound given that these were natural processes, but mindful of Japanese customs, he was ashamed not to. And so he sent Yosa out for socks, listened in the corridor for the sound of the lift doors closing, and only then did he undo his belt and go into the bathroom.

Gilbert, his torso bare, was towel-drying his hair when Yosa arrived back with the socks. He had had an extremely hot shower. Water from Japanese showers came out practically boiling. For the sake of the ascetic practices on which they were about to embark, he had set the highest possible temperature he could endure, and the skin over his entire body had turned a crab red. It reminded him of those monkeys with the pink rumps, Japanese macaques who always look so appealing in the tourist brochures, the way they bathe in the hot springs in deep winter. Monkeys with red faces, surrounded in steam. Steam was rising off him too, a steam body, a boiled red monkey. He quickly threw on a T-shirt and reached out for the new socks. When Yosa wasn't looking he pressed his hot face to them and wistfully sniffed them, because they were so new, so unused, so fresh. Gilbert would have quite liked to have seen some Japanese macaques; perhaps a surreptitious reason for his trip was so he would get to see animals, foreign creatures like the Japanese raccoon dog that resembled the American raccoon or the European badger, mythical white foxes that could metamorphose into gentlewomen and graceful young men, even brown bears in the impenetrable wilderness of Hokkaidō, a childish longing, a stubborn hope that he believed had been lost forever. He above all wanted to see the macaques in the snowy water baths – it would have been better if he had come in winter and not late summer, as he wanted to see how these animals made their way through the landscape, what traces they left behind, he wanted to see what inquisitiveness motivated them. Crab-red monkeys with bushy brown fur that exist both without question and without explanation. Animals whose movements strengthened Gilbert's own sense of existence.

He put on his shoes and picked up his bag, pawed for the key to the room. We'll begin, Gilbert said grandly, with the cherry blossoms of Ueno.

The blossoms of Ueno can't be seen at this time of year, Yosa objected as they left the hotel. Gilbert was riled. This Japanese man just didn't get it. He was slipshod when it was a matter of careful planning, he was too particular when flexibility was required, another reason for his failure.

We're going to Ueno, Gilbert explained patiently, and we'll visualize the blossom that Bashō would have seen. It's not about the blossom per se, it's about the energy of the place. Seeing as Bashō's journey took place five hundred years ago, it cannot be a decisive factor whether we're writing in spring or autumn. The time has passed, the place remains.

You couldn't tell from Yosa's expression whether he had understood the argument. But his body tightened up, casting off the exhaustion, and he took on the dependable, attentive demeanour of a tour guide.

In Ueno Park he steered Gilbert along the central avenue, which was indeed filled with a considerable number of cherry trees, and the light fell so dappled on their leaves that for a moment Gilbert could almost believe he was seeing a sea of white blossom. Or snow. Either would have been preferable to this insipid green; even when it was all about the place and not about the time, he couldn't take the slightest pleasure in the cherry trees. When faced with the blossom, even Bashō himself could only recall one line of Saigyō on the day he set off on his journey: *When will I see them again?*

Gilbert for his part vaguely recalled a different poem where it states that splitting open the cherry tree in order to find the blossom is the wrong approach. He turned around, stamped off back to the station without waiting for Yosa, and took it upon himself to completely disregard the subject of cherry blossoms for the rest of the journey and, for reasons of efficiency, logistics, and the season, to instead concentrate on the hardy evergreen pines.

Kita-Senju Station. Suicide spot. Faceless high-rises. Wide streets, never-ending traffic. Not a trace of a historic post station, where travellers could rest. They waited for a long time at a crossing. Then the lights suddenly turned green. They couldn't decide whether to cross or not. After the third green phase Yosa reluctantly jumped into action, crossing over to a row of houses of which only their rear exits and the ugly boxes of the air conditioning units were visible. They walked flanked by these boxes that rhythmically reoccurred as if there were only one of them, stuck in a time loop walking past the same one over and over again. Then there were the abandoned restaurants offering dusty plastic versions of their set menus in their front windows. A small supermarket, a shop selling sports trophies. As if sleepwalking, Yosa sought out a brand-new building, barely larger than a kiosk. They entered through the glass door into a crowded space. Two customers, a screen, and a stool were all that could be accommodated in this post office. Unthinkable that the historic post station had once stood in this exact place. But at least there was a post office here. They bought a single stamp with a floral motif and a picture postcard, and Gilbert wrote Mathilda only a single line: *Hi from Tokyo*.

They continued down the main street, Yosa unswerving, Yosa automaton-like, Yosa mute. The dead-straight street rose into a bridge over the Sumida River. Yosa led them to the riverbank.

Blackened surface of the water, shielded by the arc of the bridge, utterly smooth, like the granite floor of a bank.

This is where Bashō and his travelling companion came to shore, Yosa explained tersely. They completed the first stage of their journey by boat. This is where they moored.

This place – Gilbert recognized at first glance – was perfect for Yosa's intentions. Motionless water that, no matter what one threw into it, would immediately find its way back to its motionless state and would cover up everything that had come to pass with its indifferent slickness. They leaned on the rail and watched the water. It reflected the bridge's frame, reflected its white-and-turquoise coating, strangely childish pastel colours like those one often finds in places of social crises, in clinics and care homes, in order to compensate for the nameless catastrophes with an inoffensive colour scheme. Pillars the shade of mint stuck out from the silkiness of the river, rosy buoys bobbed like lost heads, gaudy struts crossed one another to form a structure made from plastic toys and ice cream. Up top, the bridge's steel girder arched like the track of a roller coaster.

Gilbert turned around, wanting to leave. That's when he saw Bashō. Life-sized Bashō, a graffito painted on the wall of the riverbank, Bashō as a brush painting in the style of the Edo period, Bashō with his travelling companion getting ready to scale the riverbank to seek out his lodgings for the night, bringing the first day of travelling to an end.

Gilbert had imagined Bashō to be a little more impressive. He found this depiction sobering. A weedy, hunched figure, umbrellaed by a broad pilgrim's hat, the straps of the pilgrim's bag weighing down his neck, his frame held up by the crutch-like pilgrim's staff. Bashō, followed by an even more weighed-down companion, indeed he was practically crawling along the floor. He had the back of his head to any onlookers. His face could not be seen.

Yosa had nodded almost imperceptibly, allowed Gilbert to go ahead of him, and they climbed the steps one after the other up to the street.

And now? Yosa asked. He hadn't asked very loudly. He would never dare let such a question, one expressing a certain indecision, if not downright dissatisfaction, thereby openly placing Gilbert's powers of decision making into question, slip out of his mouth, but his upright posture had wilted a little, his body had slumped infinitesimally, he turned one way and then the other, as if he didn't know what to do anymore – in short, he radiated impatience.

And now, Gilbert proclaimed, we will both compose a short poem.

Yosa nodded, flabbergasted. We need a table, he blurted out. For writing on.

They went to a small tavern near the mail kiosk and ate ramen. Yosa was acting sheepishly. He fished the bits of vegetables and meat out of his bowl, guzzled down the noodles, drained the broth, doing so in such a peculiar manner that it was as if he wasn't really doing it at all. They eventually finished eating. Yosa lowered his chin and directed a few words at the tabletop. Gilbert only made out a faint mumble. He couldn't stand it when his students muttered away to themselves, when they wanted to say something without actually saying it, as if using this tactic would absolve them from the obligation of being right or wrong. He made an effort not to snap at Yosa, he made an effort just as he always did on campus, to ask him kindly and patiently to repeat what he had said, and loudly and clearly this time. Yosa slumped in his seat, shrunk himself to a microscopic tininess, and raised his voice an almost imperceptible shade louder. The Bashō locations in the Greater Tokyo Area, he said just audibly, are worthless now. There's no point visiting them, the modern age has left them in its wake and spoiled their beauty.

Gilbert was rendered speechless. Who did this Japanese youth think he was? Was he criticizing him? Presumably he had no imagination whatsoever.

Gilbert gave a speech on modern Tokyo, on Old Edo, outlining how the city had transformed over the centuries, how the high-rises had sprouted up, how the whole region had been drowned in a twinkling sea of lights, how an entirely new kind of beauty had emerged, which Bashō had obviously not lived to see – but which he certainly would have had something to say about. Gilbert stabbed his chopsticks irritably into the empty bowl, spoke about Tokyo's metamorphosis as if he had witnessed it himself. Yosa made himself very small, but Gilbert couldn't tell how much he had understood of his speech. His

English, he recalled, was atrocious. And an assertion such as this one – that Bashō's locations were now worthless – must have taken him hours of silent preparation; he had managed to compose a sentence in his mind in English, learn it off by heart, and say it out of the blue, at an inappropriate moment, and not without stammering and stuttering. This is what made conversing with him so tedious, so demanding.

When the bowls had been cleared away, Gilbert drew out his notebook.

Hi from Tokyo – he began, considered this for a while, and then impatiently tore a page from his notebook, which he foisted upon Yosa. He respectfully accepted the slip of paper, twisted the cap off his disposable brush, and changed his posture to start writing. It was safe to assume that Yosa had been doing this kind of thing since time immemorial.

> *Hi from Tokyo –*
> *cherry trees no longer bloom,*
> *only bare concrete.*

Gilbert read his poem through a few times and concluded that he had reached the heart of the matter. The rules of the haiku, which he had learnt from the appendix of the Bashō book, had been perfectly realized within these lines: five, then seven, then once more five syllables, an allusion to the season, a sensuous impression, universal and seemingly impersonal, in which a sensitive reader would have nevertheless been able to decipher profound emotion.

Yosa wrote:

Former post station –
farewell to white envelopes,
blossoms of summer.

Yosa's poem, Gilbert had to admit, did show traditional meth-
ods. He had succeeded in alluding to the relevant line from
Saigyō that Bashō had quoted in this very same place – a literary
device that showed wide reading and intellectual sophistica-
tion. Nevertheless, the young man had clung to his own subject
– the suicide note – inasmuch as the text revealed its full meaning only to those persons privy and was, strictly speaking, a
fluke. At least Yosa had managed to put something down on
paper. Bashō's companion Sora had also been a poet, and
during their journey to the north he had contributed one or
two haiku to Bashō's diary.

With his spirits lifted, Gilbert ordered dessert. Scoops of ice
cream flavoured with matcha tea. Yosa praised the ice cream,
praised the quality of the tea powder used to make it, claimed
that he could clearly taste that the tea had originated in the Uji
region. Then as he praised something or other else, praising
himself into a kind of frenzy, his stuck-on beard came loose at
one corner, and Yosa, without toning down his facial expres-
sions, simply pressed it back down.

On the way to Ueno Park, Yosa had seen a poster showing
a famous kabuki actor. This actor was performing that day in

Tokyo, not far from the hotel, in a few hours, very soon. A performance, Yosa said, that would be authentic, traditional, one that Bashō would have also appreciated.

Gilbert considered this reference to Bashō's taste crude, but Yosa was clearly missing the vocabulary he needed to be able to express the outstanding qualities of the actor another way. Gilbert was worn out – he would have preferred to have travelled back to the hotel and lain down for a while. Sending the young Japanese man off to the theatre alone, however, seemed too much of a risk.

At twelve noon they were standing in the queue for the ticket office at the kabuki theatre in Ginza and shuffling past an advertising display. The posters depicted a young woman with her hair pinned up and adorned with flowers, her face painted white like a mask. Yosa was nodding his head ecstatically, bobbing it about like one of those clockwork ducks from Gilbert's childhood, and it appeared that he was shaking his small backside underneath his trench coat. He was drawing attention to himself, and Gilbert, surrounded by stoic Japanese accustomed to restraining themselves in every aspect of their lives, felt ashamed of him. How could a potential suicide case let himself get worked up into a wild state of joyous expectation at the sight of the blossom-bedecked, gaudily outfitted lady on the poster? It was incomprehensible. Gilbert paid for the tickets, he paid for the incredibly expensive tickets with an unmoving face like he had an infinite supply of Japanese yen, and because there was still time before the performance was starting, Yosa led them into the theatre's café and ordered tea.

Gilbert, who had committed himself to not liking tea, drank it skeptically in tiny sips. He couldn't identify an unpleasant flavour. In fact, the tea didn't taste of anything at all.

Yosa marvelled at the tea bowl, which had a stylized theatre mask painted on the bottom of the inside. A white face, distorted in divine indignation, with narrow eye slits and broad strokes of red on the cheekbones and temples. The positive Hero, Yosa explained, made up in auspicious, righteous red, while the Villain has thick blue veins running across his face, signifying his cold-blooded nature. Gilbert scrutinized his own bowl more closely; it too showed a kabuki mask, but the colour of the tea had mixed with the base colour of the mask, so that he couldn't be sure whether it revealed a hero or an anti-hero. He drank up his tea – the colour of the mask remained a nondescript brownish. The role of the Demon, said Yosa. And then he set about explaining to Gilbert that they hadn't in fact gone there for the male roles – the famous actor performing that evening was actually a master in the portrayal of young women. That was who they had seen on the poster at the entrance. He was the greatest onnagata in the country, a living national treasure who had first appeared onstage as a girl at the age of four, who had devoted his life to playing young ladies, and who, now at over sixty years of age, had surpassed every member of the female sex in gracefulness.

They found their seats, typical theatre seats covered with red velvet. The curtain was still down, the hall was filling up, usherettes made their way down the aisles holding up signs showing a crossed-out camera, a crossed-out mobile phone, a crossed-out film camera. Then a man's voice rang out from the loudspeakers, which, according to Yosa, explained the program, walked them through the plot, and alluded to the highlights of the show. An English-language program wouldn't have hurt, in Gilbert's opinion. He had to piece together a coherent plot from Yosa's broken translation.

A girl is betrayed by her beloved. She dies of grief and is born again as a crane, as a bird of grace. She dies of rage and indignation and is reborn as a crane, that is, degraded. The girl should have remained calm, entered a monastery, counterbalanced the guilt of the beloved with her prayers. A girl is impatient with her beloved and is transformed into a crane as punishment. The beloved marries another, and the crane dies of grief. It might not be a crane, perhaps a completely different creature, a crow or a heron, birdlike or in any case capable of flight, an angel or a ghost.

When the curtain went up, the actor was already standing in the middle of the stage. He wore a floor-length brocaded robe with a wide cloth sash passed around his waist, an enormous bow tied at his back. The years behind the white makeup couldn't be discerned from the back of the auditorium. Delicate features, red lips, a visage of consummate elegance. He held a fan in his hand, and when it began to stir, Yosa gripped Gilbert's arm and held on to it. Gilbert stiffened, looked past Yosa, and attempted to watch the action on the stage. He made an extreme effort but was unable to determine that anything was happening at all. The actor moved at a snail's pace, turning around himself infinitely slowly, putting his foot forward once extremely cautiously, letting the fan sink a tiny fraction. If it was supposed to be a dance, it was the most tedious dance Gilbert had ever seen – no mean feat when dancing was overwhelmingly boring for the spectator in the first place. Mathilda had once coerced him into accompanying her to a ballet performance, and he swore to himself after the first ten minutes never to go again, and in case of doubt he should undermine his good nature, be tough, say no, he tormented himself through the whole one and a half hours, fidgeting in his seat, sucking on boiled sweets, and at least succeeding in making sure Mathilda never approached him with such a suggestion ever again. However, when he compared the European ballet with the Japanese kabuki dance, ballet was frankly thigh-slapping, popular, primitive entertainment. The kabuki dancer moved in millimetres, he required many minutes to open his fan even halfway, it was like watching an amoeba for entertainment, and Gilbert clawed his hand – the small, cool hand of the Japanese man clasped to it – into the armrest and bored his fingernails into the velvet.

Suddenly the curtain fell. Gilbert had managed to grasp not the slightest narrative, no progression, but Yosa relaxed, drew back his hand, and informed him that the first piece had come to an end. It had been a quarter of an hour at most, which had nevertheless felt like an infinite expanse of time. The Japanese audience members sitting around them unpacked picnics and consumed them without leaving the velvet seats. Yosa offered him a small, sweet, rubbery ball made of rice flour wrapped in a salty oak leaf. Gilbert ate the sweet, leaned back in his seat, listened to the prattling, boisterous multitude, and in a single blow he was pervaded by the tense anticipation of the audience.

The Crossroads of Illusions – this is how Bashō had felt as he bid farewell to his previous life and was resigned to the idea that he would hike 5,000 kilometres. The practice of hiking as a journey through life, meaning that one stands at the crossroads and is able to choose whether one goes or stays, whether one keeps dreaming the dream one is currently dreaming or exchanges it for a different one. And, according to the teaching of Buddhism, when measured against the eternal truth, one choice is as unreal as the other.

Gilbert now waited for the curtain to rise again. He was ready to give up all resistance. But he primly put his hands in his lap so that Yosa was unable to touch him.

The actor was now wearing a white robe with a hood that completely covered his face. He also concealed himself behind a parasol, which he half closed, then opened again, put down in the scenery, then picked back up. It was snowing on the stage, and the actor's feet, wearing white, split-toed tabi socks, pushed through the sparse flakes; the stand where he kept placing the parasol was covered with paperboard depicting a snowdrift. The set emitted an altogether depressive atmosphere, and Gilbert wondered whether this performance was really the best thing for Yosa. He himself was now eagerly waiting for the actor to take off the hood and once more show his feminine features. The slow-motion effect, he now realized, solely served to intensify a quasi-sacred concentration. And, in fact, the hood did eventually fall back. Gilbert clenched his hands together. Eventually the white robe fell and unveiled flame-red brocade; there were multiple costume changes without a pause in the dancing, indeed there were, scurrying around the stage, two dark figures who, in their dark clothing, weren't really there at all, and who, behind the slowly rotating parasol, released the actor of the sashes, the belts, ripped the upper layers of material from his body, and then he burst out from behind the parasol in completely new garments. To Gilbert's astonishment, the costume changes took place in a matter of seconds, a real metamorphosis that called for an extraordinary amount of dexterity on behalf of the helpers and enormous agility on the part of the dancer. His respect for the performance grew, because this finesse was also manifested in the gentle, slow-motion movements. He wasn't entirely sure whether the woman onstage, whose intricate gestures he had grown to admire, should be the one he fell in love with or actually the man enacting this extraordinary control of his body, or whether he didn't much more wish to be this lithesome actor himself or, more specifically, to possess his exceptionally stunning beauty. Gilbert furtively tried to hold his own hand in such a perfectly graceful way in the dark auditorium, the way the dancer demonstrated, so utterly enticing, so convincingly feminine, which no woman on this planet would have been able to accomplish. Dear Mathilda, he formulated in the silence, it was an ambivalence that no one could match up to. No one, at any rate, who was real and alive.

When they left the theatre it was early afternoon. They squeezed themselves into the overcrowded underground carriage and got off after a few stations at the Imperial Palace Gardens, Kōkyo-Gaien, pine formations on a wide lawn. There was a giggling school group right next to them continuously sucking milk-shakes out of disposable beakers through thick plastic straws.

Touristic stomping around in Tokyo wasn't exactly what Gilbert had in mind for his abandonment of everything. Abandonment meant not following the promises of this world, and definitely not those that draw in large groups of people.

Two women in red hiking gear were taking double portraits with the aid of a selfie stick. Gilbert couldn't stand those things. He had banned his students from using them, not only during teaching time, but in general. Those who wished to learn something from him, he would always announce at the beginning of his sessions, had to be capable of leading a reasonably dignified life. This categorically excluded certain items for personal use. He naturally couldn't check who kept up to his standards. But here, among the pines, where people were messing about with telescopic sticks, especially here with the pines, he saw once more how sensible his advice had been.

The pines demanded something of their visitors. They stood peacefully and gracefully, their bundles of needles opened in patient green, lustrous coronas, a hypnotic divergence where a dancer opens a fist, relaxing and splaying their fingers. The pines stood steadily among the restless people, islands of tranquility, dignified – they had proven their worth over hundreds of years. You had to rise to their level.

Pines, as if he were seeing them for the very first time. Pines in the fierce afternoon light, a void, a nebulous black seen through incessant blinking. Pines, their shadows stretched out over the path. Gilbert stepped from one shadow trunk to another, crossed over an immaterial bridge of wooden planks, walked over an abyss too deep to arouse fear and with the appearance of having been filled in with asphalt, swimming shadows of pine needles on what appeared to be the square in front of the Imperial Palace, intangible branches, bark, pine cones; the Emperor cannot be seen, all that can be seen is his aura in the form of this army of pine trees.

Gilbert could sense the young Japanese man at his side, who was thankful for the bare minimum of encouragement, and who in this moment seemed even more incorporeal than the shadow of a pine tree. Yosa pointed out that each individual pine tree was carefully pruned into shape.

The imperial pines could be classified by their aesthetic appearances, just as one does with a bonsai. Chokkan – a formal upright trunk that tapers off at the top and is uniformly green. Mōyogi – an informal upright trunk bent into an S-shape. Shakkan – a perfectly straight trunk tilted to one side at a forty-five-degree angle, as if the tree could fall at any moment. Gilbert liked Sōkan – the double trunk, forking off in different directions. He found these trees the most generous, whereas the others were thin like giant chopsticks stuck in the ground and also too meagrely needled for his liking. Bundles of needles tallied up at the ends of hyper-controlled branches, condensed into which was the untameable beauty this country was so famous for. Out of politeness he tried to focus on each tree individually and to reverently nod every time, just as he observed the older Japanese couples doing, as they sauntered along the path, topped with battered sun hats, truly absorbed in the contemplation of the pines. Now and again Gilbert believed someone would be pointing at a specific branch, but perhaps they were pointing at something completely different, seeing as he couldn't make out any special features on whatever branch it was. Yosa, however, appeared to follow the pointing with his eyes, and Gilbert, walking beside him, sensed from the tensing of his body that he straightened himself up with each one of these gazes and inwardly straightened up too, as if he were mimicking the disposition of the pines and gaining new energy from the sight of them.

Fukinagashi, the windswept form, which grows to the side facing away from the weather; Kengai, the cascade, where the tree bows down into the depths from a rocky outcrop, like Bunjingi, the form of the literati, which is characterized by the fact that the pines appeared rather worn, grew irregularly, were somewhat debarked, and therefore looked particularly old and natural – they would, without a doubt, according to Yosa, come upon this tree form in Matsushima.

They returned to the hotel early in the evening. Yosa warmed a bottle of sake in the electric kettle and poured hot water over instant noodles. They felt too exhausted to go out and get a decent meal or to even sit at a table in the hotel restaurant. They packed their bags for the next morning and prematurely lay down to sleep. Gilbert turned out the light. Then he got back out of bed, pulled open the curtains, and stared for a long time at the colourful neon signs in nighttime Tokyo from his bed.

Just as Gilbert was about to fall asleep, Yosa started talking.

He had gone out with a girl only once. He had invited her to a traditional restaurant. They sat on tatami mats next to a darkly lacquered folding screen that partitioned off their nook from the rest of the diners, and that was so smoothly polished it was almost a mirror. Because the girl was so pretty, he didn't dare look at her, and only looked at the shimmer of her reflected in the screen. When she got up to go to the restroom and her skirt swung around her bony knees, he saw in the reflection that the skirt was in flames. He ought to have been suspicious at this point, if not much earlier, he ought to have realized that she was a fox that had taken the form of a girl. Foxes are masters of transformation and are capable of all kinds of magic tricks. They can start a fire with their snout or the tip of their tail, they can create delusions and spark obsession. The flaming skirt was a clear sign, but Yosa followed the movement of her legs with such a burning fascination that he wrote it off as an optical illusion caused by emotional confusion.

They spoke very little that evening. They ate a lot: squid and tuna, sliced lotus root and black, sprout-shaped seaweed, jellyfish salad. They ate soup and meatballs, salted plums and tofu skin crisped up like bark. Deepwater prawns, scallops, sweet fried tofu parcels filled with rice and sesame seeds.

Yosa didn't dare strike up a conversation, so he sat with his head bowed over his food, looked embarrassedly at the tabletop, at the dishes, at the gleaming screen. The girl was waiting for him to broach a topic, for him to lead the conversation so it would be possible for her to steady his flow of words with a broad spectrum of validating noises, as the conventional roles dictated. She commentated on the mussels with ah and oh and yesyes, nodded after every piece of fish, but since he just couldn't get going she made her own attempts after a while. She posed him questions about his eating preferences, his music taste, his hobbies, the most harmless of queries, but Yosa wasn't capable of responding to her prompts. His mouth felt parched even though he was endlessly drinking tea, he gave one-word answers, shovelled down huge quantities of rice, ordered more dishes, watched out of the corner of his eye the way she lightly held the chopsticks, stayed silent. In the end she began to talk about herself, perhaps in order to salvage the evening, or perhaps because he was apparently a good listener and she thought she understood him. She was wrong on this point, because he indeed was listening, but he was barely able to grasp the meaning of what was being said, and he could now remember only fragments of one of the anecdotes she told.

Her parents had just had their new car blessed, and her brother had driven and totalled the car the very next day. He had been extremely lucky to have survived, he hadn't sustained any serious injuries, but she now questioned her parents' beliefs, doubted the worth of a Shintō ritual that must have been quite expensive and ought to have warded off accidents happening to vehicles and their passengers. Had her parents made a mistake by not having her brother present at the ceremony, while she had been standing beside them in the parking lot, had endured the bowing and put up with all of it – could it be possible that her parents had given too little money, had she not taken it seriously enough, the recitations and the singing, the hitting of the gong, the stroking of the vehicle with a bushel of white paper strips, the handing over of the consecrated plaque?

She was struggling with who she was, with the world, basically the usual problems with religious tradition that inevitably arose around that age; in retrospect, Yosa recognized that this speech was meant to make him feel at ease, to imply a student-like normality, because when they kissed one another goodbye that evening, or more accurately, when she unexpectedly and briskly touched her lips against his own, the flames flared up once more, burning his mouth. The fox snout sent the burning coursing through his whole body, and he was suddenly certain about what was going on, because he had never experienced such a substantial burn before. He pushed her away from him, turned around, and ran away, in a direction that wasn't even homeward, just away, and when he turned back one more time, he didn't see her tan skirt, or her white stockings, but an over-sized fox tail disappearing around the corner of the street.

They went to the same school, but from then on he acted as though he couldn't see her. His parents found his behaviour inexcusable, the parents of the girl were mortified, and the whole school was whispering about what had happened, so that it would have been for the best if he had just jumped from a bridge at the time. But in his confusion, he found himself unable to make any decision whatsoever.

When he began his university studies, he left the family home and moved to a different city, and even though it was an extremely humiliating experience, he had been grateful for a little space. He had turned down taking over the tea shop, hoping to start a new life. Nevertheless, he couldn't stop think-ing about her. No other woman had aroused his interest. He was obsessed, enamoured with the fox spirit.

Gilbert sighed. What should he tell the boy? His students beat themselves up with comparable emotional states, but they weren't so dogged about it, they loosened up a bit and were much more patient with themselves. And they didn't camouflage their inhibitions with such flowery language. They knew what things were, they knew in almost unhealthy amounts, which didn't solve their difficulties, and in fact often made them far more complicated, but this being in the know at least gave them perspective, helped them reach a state of partial apathy that made it possible for them to let unpleasant things wash over them.

Why didn't Yosa have even a minimal amount of Buddhist composure, why wasn't he even the teensiest bit mellow, as one ought to expect from the land of Zen, and where was the almost pornographic eagerness to experiment, whereby the Japanese reputedly succeed in integrating even the crudest obscenities into an excessive sex life without the slightest feelings of guilt?

Tell me more about foxes, he finally said into the room's dimness, into the ever-flickering lights, domineering, mysterious, shrill. He wanted to try the pastoral mode, which involved meeting people at their level, a rhetorical technique that he had always found intolerable because it meant lowering the general standard to the lowest possible degree. The boy, sensitive and easily offended, seemed capable of anything, and it was important not to embarrass him.

Foxes, Yosa explained obligingly, acquire their magical capabilities with increasing age. They prefer taking on the shape of people who are wealthy and seductive – qualities that foxes apparently find most agreeable in humans. The more experienced and powerful they are, the greater the number of tails they have. They are always hungry and eat vast quantities of food. Most often they induce their transformation by placing a green leaf on their head.

Super, Gilbert said. He was unbelievably tired. We'll talk about it more in the morning. Yosa might like to consider whether he had caught the girl with a leaf on her head or even in the vicinity of leaves.

He could hear from Yosa's breathing that he hadn't caught this instruction and had finally fallen asleep. Gilbert drew the curtains and locked out the colourful flickering. The darkness was now dense, and he waited to sink into it. He thought of leaves, colourful autumn leaves and green leaves, of Mathilda beneath bushy branches, he saw swirling leaves in the darkness, swirling trees, the vast forests of Pennsylvania.

Red maple. Silver maple. Sugar maple. Moose maple. Vermont maple. Sycamore maple. American plane. Flowering dogwood. Tamarack larch. Weymouth pine.

Table Mountain pine. Pitch pine. Virginia red cedar. Pennsylvanian ash. Red oak. White ash. Cucumber magnolia. Black tupelo. Redbuds. Sassafras. White poplar. Aspen. Black poplar. American beech. Virginian hornbeam. American hornbeam. Black cherry. Mountain black cherry. Bird cherry. Paper birch. Black birch. Gold birch. River birch. Canoe birch. Swamp birch. Hawthorn. American elm. Slippery elm. Red mulberry. Black oak. Northern red oak. White oak. Pin oak. Scarlet oak. Chestnut oak. Tulip poplar. Black willow. Witch hazel. Robinia. Copper beech. Bitternut. Mockernut hickory. Pignut hickory. Black walnut. Crab apple. Persimmon. Hemlock. Balsam fir. Canadian spruce. Common pawpaw. Horse chestnut. Sweet chestnut. A row of alders.

They stood at the edge of the alder swamp. A single leaf came free and sailed between the branches, until at last it landed on the median.

Enveloping dusk, the insinuation of evening. Stormy clouds move eastward, looming and as choppy as the sea, grey rolls of it wheeled onward by the wind, piling up like unending traffic, the rumbling highway, the heart of America. Clouds with breasts and battlements, mammatus, castellanus, a huge fortress built from a glistening swarm of jellyfish, they glide overhead, slide by, the jellyfish swirl with their cloudy backs, strands of them break free, stratus fractus, take on a life of their own beneath the oppressive blanket, nimbostratus, it will rain soon.

SENDAI

The next morning, his head was still brimming with foliage – a sack packed tightly with dried leaves. He felt hollow, hollow and weak, as if he were recuperating after a long illness, or as if the oppressive force relentlessly fuelling him had decided to take a break for a while.

Tokyo – Ueno – Ōmiya – Utsunomiya – Kōriyama – Fukushima – Sendai …

Everything had already begun to change as they boarded the high-speed train *Mountain Echo* in Tokyo, heading for Sendai, as if Tokyo were the pivot around which the whole country tipped from the familiar into the unknown. While the train they had taken back from the suicide forest and which bore the name *Light* had been very full and – in spite of its brand-new furnishings, loud upholstery, and the latest technology – somewhat uncomfortable, the train to Sendai was carrying only a few passengers. And as they travelled north via Ichinoseki and Kitakami toward Morioka, the train would empty out further. In Morioka, travellers wanting to reach Hokkaidō and the northernmost Japanese islands changed trains. Aomori, Noboribetsu, Sapporo – this was the route that lead to Kamchatka, to the Kuril Islands along the Russian border. Yellowish curtains swayed at the windows, barely keeping out the sun; the other train had had thick plastic blinds. The antique curtains signalled the start of a journey into Bashō's north, the path of the adventurer and the pilgrim, the yearning, the resolute – was it still?

They sat on the train as the landscape slid easily by, leaving station after station in their wake. Stationary travelling, action without action. Or a dull, unconscious drifting, like tattered leaves on the wind.

They were on a direct route to Matsushima, no beating about the bush, no layovers. This meant that they skipped some of Bashō's stations. Muro no Yashima, where the protective patron god of Fuji, the Goddess of the Blooming Cherry Tree, was enshrined, the temple complex at Nikkō, and the ancient willow tree in Ashino, which the monk Saigyō had already documented in poetry centuries before.

In Nikkō, Bashō composed a haiku about nothing more than the vernal green of the new leaf:

> *See this holy site –*
> *tender, light green leaves of spring,*
> *shone through with sunlight.*

Young foliage, illuminated by the sun – the whole of the temple grounds lit up for him in this image, though of course one needed to know that the name of the temple complex itself means 'it shines like the sun.' Bashō's haiku is therefore a spiritual simile. Just as the sun shines through the leaves, the spiritual power of the temple shines through the world, through its people. Leaves, young and vulnerable on the branch, penetrated by the almighty sun. Gilbert already felt like a loose leaf anyway, so there wasn't much to be gained in Nikkō. More importantly it was vital to set some parameters for the journey, and he had set them: they had been tirelessly occupying themselves with pines for days and couldn't devote themselves to the innumerable deciduous trees along the route as well.

As far as the ancient willow at Ashino was concerned, both Saigyō and Bashō hid in its shade while life went on around them. The tree provided them with a symbol of mental tranquility in the face of the fleeting nature of the world.

Saigyō wrote one of the most famous waka poems under the willow in Ashino:

> At the trail's edge,
> where a crystal-clear brook flows
> in the willow's shade
> I wished to pause, so remained
> in this place for a while.

Bashō thought of himself as someone engaged in a poetic dialogue with the great poet Saigyō. That Saigyō was long dead didn't trouble him: it was a communication between immortal spirits. Thrilled to have the privilege of sitting in the shade of the same tree, he wrote the following:

A whole rice field
will have been planted before
I leave the willow.

Another example, if there weren't already enough, of the lack of consistency present in all poetry. At times the tree stands for that which is transient, thereby emphasizing eternity, yet at other times it stands for the everlasting in the middle of constant change – it was the one and the other, it was a contradiction in itself. It irritated Gilbert, and he would have liked to have asked Yosa how he felt about it, was it a contradiction, was it a paradox, was it perhaps obvious for a Japanese person, as with a rather easy kōan that only a non-Japanese person wouldn't be able to solve?

Meanwhile, they had roared on past the willow, sailed on past the willow; they had skipped the tender leaves of spring, they had thus far been unable to find peace in the face of fleeting things.

Dear Mathilda,

We're taking a shortcut. If we made a stop for every distraction, we'd never reach the pine islands. We will definitely not be travelling to Mount Mihara. Yosa is extremely upset about this and won't talk to me. For centuries the world-weary have ascended the volcano and thrown themselves into the crater. The catalyst for this was a novel, a bestseller, in which a couple in an ill-fated love affair settle on this exact idea, and everyone has been aping them ever since – the Werther effect. Tourism to the island grew disproportionately after the book came out.

Special ferry services were set up so the suicidal could reach their end in comfort and so sightseers could be transported as well, entire families spent weekends walking along the newly laid-out hiking trails to the most spectacular parts of the island, and even if the crater has been fenced off in the meantime, its popularity has been hardly affected at all. Between 1930 and 1937, over 2,000 people are thought to have jumped from one of the observation points into the smouldering lava. I don't want Yosa to have to endure seeing a mass grave, and I have practically forbidden him from seeing it.

We will also be leaving out the Sesshōseki, a rock of volcanic origin that Bashō visited during his journey. Noxious fumes rise from it, annihilating all life in its general vicinity. It is permanently topped by a thick layer of dead insects. Dazed birds fall from the sky, mammals avoid getting too close to it, plants wither away, so the stone sits in a barren wasteland surrounded by scree, asserting its solitary reign. A gloomy place eternally submerged in oppressive fog, a lost place where nothing of worth can be found. Only tourists come near it, flocking there in droves. That the murderous vapours would tempt Yosa is certainly plausible. I too would be interested in this kind of phenomenon if I were his age and in such a desperate state. Shove the swarms of perished bees and flies out of the way with my foot and attempt to inhale the fumes. What had convinced me to steer clear of the stone, however, was an annotation in Bashō's travelogue. For a long time, the stone has been considered the

manifestation of the nine-tailed fox, a powerful demoness
who at the end of her career, after she had ruined the
Emperor by masquerading as his beloved, transformed
into this toxic boulder. Even if the stone has been exor-
cised in the meantime and the fox's spirit has been extin-
guished, the emanation of the fumes has in no way
diminished. I think it's for the best to keep people like
Yosa, people who clearly have at best an ambivalent rela-
tionship with fox-like figures – whether they exist or not
– far away from this troublesome place. Taking into
account Yosa's special psychic disposition, we will instead,
and I want to put my whole energy behind this, spare
ourselves some physical exertion and instead approach
the Sesshōseki via the narrow path of poetry.

Gilbert thought that what he had already drafted was pretty good. He scratched out an English translation beside his poem and held it out to Yosa.

The poisonous stone –
its vapours transporting me
back to ancient times.

Yosa, huddled in his seat, seemed to read his thoughts and disapproved. Yosa endeavoured through the overpowering emissions of an aura of discontent not only to read his thoughts, but to manipulate them. He wordlessly urged Gilbert to disembark the train at the poisonous stone. He haughtily closed his eyes against the verdurous, resplendent landscape and refused to take in the banality of the outdoors. When he didn't get his own way, he sulked like a toddler. No wonder his parents despaired of him.

Yosa stubbornly sucked on the end of his brush for a long time. Nothing came to mind, he didn't want to do it, he found the whole task ridiculous, beneath him. Finally he wrote:

In the harsh wasteland
I withhold myself from you …
petrified vixen.

Yosa's poem seemed too subjective to Gilbert and showed a lack of grammatical clarity, at least as far as he could make out from the German translation reconstructed from the English translation of the Japanese. It was down to the ellipsis after 'you,' which substituted meaningful punctuation with meagre vagueness. If one were to have proceeded with a comma, which had been neglected or disguised in this case, one would read 'petrified vixen' as an extension of 'you,' and the lyrical 'I' would be a counterparty to the fox. If, however, one were to insert a dash instead of a comma (a popular technique in German) in order to show a mental turn of thought in the course of the haiku, this would make possible the reading that the lyrical 'I' had itself transformed into a fox out of wounded devotion – or had at least threatened to do so. This indecisiveness seemed to Gilbert to be illustrative of Yosa's condition, and once more showed that mental lucidity and emotional stability were the conditions *sine quibus non* for composing a haiku. Yosa regrettably lacked both.

The outer suicide and the inner suicide, he said to Yosa, are completely different things. Bashō strove for the inner suicide, he wanted to be free of his ego in order to be freed up for his poetry. This could be seen as unnecessarily extreme, but it would be the far more interesting experiment.

Yosa didn't answer. Yosa was pretending he couldn't hear anything and couldn't see anything.

He sat slumped in his seat, utterly resistant, utterly rigid, a burdensome vow never to yield, no matter what forces were placed upon him. The force might be an extraordinary one: it might for example be the authoritative Gilbertian force of a university lecturer, a force of wisdom and pedagogy, a force that, viewed from a purely spiritual perspective, was of an unsurpassable older man, a force that a young Japanese man couldn't compete with – there was nothing for him to do except bow to it over and over again. A force, therefore, that came close to omnipotence. But the Japanese man only bowed superficially, he bowed in such an exaggerated manner – twisted, clenched, folded in on himself, immensely compacted to his core – that he asserted a hidden gravity, all designed precisely to puncture such omnipotence.

'Can an all-powerful being create a stone so heavy it cannot even lift the stone itself?'

The omnipotence paradox is a challenge to the idea of divine supremacy. How can we comprehend God's power, what consequences does it hold for us, are there limits to its scope? A conservative response to the paradox acknowledges simply that God could create the tremendously heavy stone but would have to concede defeat to it just like an ordinary weightlifter.

Either way – should he succeed in lifting it, then the stone is, so to speak, hollow and reveals his incompetence. Should he not succeed, he proves himself to be a failure. As far as they go, these thoughts are without doubt rational and convincing. However, the omnipotence paradox at its core isn't about the weight of the stone, but about the weight of God. Even if it contradicted everything he had ever published on the theme of God's beard, Gilbert was secretly an adherent of the concept of absolute power. Obviously, an all-powerful being could create all kinds of stones, it would be able to lift stones and simultaneously not be able to lift them, and whoever put forward the argument that a stone an all-powerful being wasn't able to lift would be physical proof contrary to his omnipotence simply hadn't understood that it wasn't about that at all, the lifting or not lifting of a stone, because the absolute power easily overrides the rules of logic that were the problem in the first place. What it really came down to (and Gilbert already understood this when he was a student of Yosa's age) was treating the omnipotence paradox as one does a piece of poetry – to recite it while not thinking logically in the slightest, to let it affect you and to simply accept it in all its striking, irrational beauty.

Yosa sat silently in his seat like a mortally offended stone.

If this Japanese man, with whom he had spent several days, had at least been schooled in the Japanese tradition of kōan, he would have been able to discuss all of these questions with him. Gilbert would come at him with riddle-like anecdotes from Yosa's own cultural sphere, which might be more familiar to him, which might make him see sense.

The kōan 'The Stone Mind,' for instance:

A Chinese Zen teacher asked two travelling monks:

'Do you consider that stone over there to be inside or outside your mind?' One of the monks answers: 'As everything is of the mind, I would say that the stone is inside my mind.' The Zen master responds: 'Your head must be very heavy if you carry a stone like that around in your mind.'

Or 'The Foreigner Has No Beard':

A monk saw a picture of the long-bearded Bodhidharma and he complained: 'Why doesn't that fellow have a beard?'

Tokyo – Ueno – Ōmiya – Utsunomiya – Kōriyama – Fukushima – Sendai …

They passed through Fukushima at super-express speed, through the mainland, far from the coast, away from the evacuated zone. There were no indicators that one of the most devastating catastrophes in Japanese history had taken place here just a few years before. The train sped past fields, past acoustic fencing, past nondescript residential neighbourhoods, past lone houses that appeared as if glued to the forested slopes. There were no cooling towers, no nuclear power stations, no ships beached far inland, no devastated houses coated in silt, no flipped cars with tires still spinning emptily in the air, no black plastic sacks filled with contaminated earth and piled up for kilometres and kilometres and never collected for disposal.

The train passed through Fukushima on a broad, indeterminate plain that looked the same as everywhere else in Japan, perhaps somewhat duller, somewhat less lovely or wildly romantic than other parts of the country, where one traversed deep canyons on narrow bridges and then raced through long tunnels. There wasn't that much in particular to see in Fukushima, and this testified to the classical traditions of East Asian countries, where the void, the bland and the reserved, was actually an aesthetic quality in itself.

Gilbert travelled during these days as if it were winter. The high summer was passing into autumn, the thermometer still neared thirty degrees Celsius every day, and yet it seemed to him as if it wasn't dry plains that he could see through the window but rather fields glittering with frost. Time and time again the impression of a wintry journey glided into his mind's eye, and he wasn't able to see the landscape as it was: hot and sharply spotlighted in sunlight, rich in detail, and close-up. The landscape threw back the dazzling light, and everywhere he saw this blazing brilliance, he saw snow.

At Sendai he vacated the cool tube of the air-conditioned super-express train and stepped down shivering onto the platform. The moist heat closed in around him like a thick robe, taking his breath away and immediately isolating him from his surroundings. Gilbert alighted with the secret desire to turn away from everything, he alighted with the fear that this turning away could actually happen, he alighted with the hope of finding something in this dislocation that would open his eyes once and for all about the nature of things. He thought primarily about pines while doing so, he thought almost exclusively about pines. The Japanese pines on their scenic island – were they truly capable of teaching him to see something? And if they were, why couldn't a completely normal pine, like one in the Brandenburg Forest, for instance, not be just as qualified to do so?

He looked around for Yosa, who had been standing next to him a moment before. Gilbert had stepped down onto the platform first, followed by Yosa, Gilbert had sensed him at his back. Then Yosa had stepped toward him and respectfully waited to see whether Gilbert had noticed the way for the disembarking passengers to exit and continue their journey. Gilbert had stood motionless in the heat, for only a few seconds, and Yosa had been swallowed up by the crowd.

Gilbert stepped to the side to allow other passengers past him, his gaze passing over their faces as he searched for Yosa's. The Japanese had stopped looking all alike to him a long time ago, but he couldn't find Yosa's face anywhere.

They were supposed to change trains here, and Gilbert looked for the way to the lower levels. Over the entrance to the main concourse was an illuminated screen depicting a bamboo forest. Electronic birdsong came from all sides, and as he descended the steps into the cool forest, the singing transformed into rice cakes and gaudy jelly cubes, into ornamental fruit made of sugar on long tables surrounded by crowds of schoolchildren in black-and-white uniforms.

Sendai Station: gigantic, modern, squeaky clean. A pineapple-yellow plastic egg the size of an airport concourse wrapped around glinting stone floors, stylish waiting areas, cavernous washrooms. Gilbert would have liked to have sat himself down at one of the groups of seats and waited awhile to see if Yosa re-emerged, just sat there and waited. A Japanese family were sitting very upright in the comfortable seats around a picnic table drinking green tea and eating rice balls topped with tiny dried fish. Gilbert sat at a table near them for a few minutes, sipped a little cold tea from his flask, and watched how they put the leftover rice balls, still wrapped in foil, into a wooden box and tied the box with a colourful cloth. All of this took place almost soundlessly, amid muted conversations and considered movements. There was no sense of the usual hectic pace one is accustomed to at train stations; this Japanese family's perform-ance was suffused with the kind of studied elegance one begins practising in earliest childhood.

In the washrooms, too, the atmosphere was akin to that of a luxury hotel. Marble and mirrors, exotic flowers, perfume. A long row of lavish sinks under lighting that made even Gilbert's face appear noble in the mirror. No droplets of water splashed around the basins, no crumpled paper towels, no little puddles on the floor. Instead there were extremely spacious cubicles with photoelectric sensors, artificial intelligence. Doors opened of their own volition, water ran when it was required, everything could be used without touching anything. He washed his hands for a long time and considered the fresh lotus blossom next to the tap, which was doubled in the mirror and became a never-ending chain of blossoms in the row of mirrors behind him.

Sendai wasn't an attractive destination. Sendai was nothing. In the travel guides, Sendai was insignificant, which meant tourists didn't go there. Remarking that one had travelled to Tokyo could, especially from a European perspective, considerably enhance one's travel history. One travelled to Sendai only if it was unavoidable, for professional or family reasons, or while in transit. And yet Gilbert had remained completely indifferent to Tokyo. Nothing sparked in his imagination when someone said 'Tokyo,' the sequence 'Tokyo – Paris – New York' left him cold, and even back in Germany he had never harboured ambitions to travel there. Sendai, on the other hand: vapid photographs on web pages, grey high-rises that might just as well be in Calcutta, in Detroit or Vladivostok. The vacuity of Sendai drew him in with a magical energy.

It was as if there were something, within this country trawled through and depicted over and over by poets for centuries, in this palimpsest of reverence and tradition, of petrified gazes and dusty stones, in the ceaseless renewal of vision, it was as if there were something in a place like Sendai that had somehow been left undiscovered.

Gilbert liked Sendai, even if all he saw of the city was the train station. Perhaps he should have stayed in Sendai, in a depressing little hotel surrounded by car parks, interchangeable buildings, flowing traffic. Wet concrete, vomit-inducing salted plums, nervous animals who can't find any garbage cans to rummage through because in this country, this country of the utmost order and cleanliness, there were no public garbage cans. He liked Sendai, a stubborn bias that he couldn't let go of for the rest of his journey.

Gilbert orbited the bright main hall several times, doing the rounds at all the stalls, peering inside every snack bar, every café. But even if Yosa had suddenly had the idea to buy something, to quickly partake of something somewhere, even if he had abruptly rushed to the washrooms, he would have come back a long time ago. And Gilbert could in no way explain how they had been so unfortunate as to lose one another at this train station.

He made his way through spacious halls and long corridors like the ones in airport terminals. He finally managed to find the right platform. It was rush hour and the platform was full. No sign of Yosa. The destinations blinked on the display board first in Japanese and then in English, they blinked lantern red, blood red on the black board, as if the desired destination was as clouded in secrecy as a Shintō god.

The Japanese were already standing in long rows behind the markings on the platform. The gentle curve of the queues was predefined by white lines on the ground. Every person abided by it with an almost tantalizing precision: the train stopped, every carriage aligned with a predetermined point on the platform, the doors opened in the empty space between the queue of people, orderly disembarking, disciplined boarding, a system so mechanized that emotions, scrambling, even out-and-out scuffles never even arose. Gilbert got into position, right at the back, and as soon as he stood in this back row he was overwhelmed by a 'me first' restlessness with a potency he had never felt before. No one lost control, everyone waited, just as they should do, they made sure not to take up too much space so as not to disturb the others, they took care not to scrape the ground with their feet or to show any other signs of impatience. Gilbert advanced by a few millimetres, practised psychic pressure through imperceptible but persistent advancement on an old woman, who after a while had no alternative but to take a small step forward and reduce the space between her and the man in front. Gilbert looked in the direction the train would be coming from every two seconds, he shifted his weight from one foot to the other, almost teetering, instead of keeping good posture with his feet together, his arms flat against his body, his face expressionless. He conducted himself in a reckless manner, and he wondered why he was behaving this way, because, really, he placed absolutely no worth on standing right at the front on the markings and feeling the looks of the others on the back of his neck. Yet he couldn't control himself; no sooner had Yosa gone than he was intentionally jostling, as if he had to give expression to what everyone else was forbidden to do.

He had queued too late and didn't get a seat. The woman in front of him had hurried to the last free place, taking it a few seconds before a schoolboy who had tried for it. But when she saw the boy hanging off the hand grip and relentlessly chatting to his friends, who had had more luck than him, she gave the seat up for him. Then she stood next to Gilbert for a long time in the packed train with an expression displaying profound offence and at the same time what could be considered an air of superiority; she had demonstrated to everyone what it meant to act selflessly, to prove courteous in every situation in life, but the boy was too gormless to appreciate what had taken place, chit-chatting with his school friends without a care in the world and not paying the old woman any further attention.

This is what ruined Japan, Gilbert could see she was thinking, this is how our morals decayed, this is how even the slightest attempt at a good upbringing vanished. He knew that she knew that he had been the one standing behind her and had exuded a certain unease, and, in spite of the train being packed, he evaded her eyes. He avoided her humble yet haughty, sanctimonious yet insulted, downcast yet merciless gaze.

They travelled underground for a long time. People disembarked at every station along the way, first the schoolchildren, then the workers, later the housewives with their shopping bags and packages. The train emptied out, at some point it became light, and they travelled in daylight through the outskirts. Industrial zones, the docks, the coast.

SHIOGAMA

Dear athilda,

We had effectively journeyed toward Matsushima without any further holdups, without delay. I did unfortunately lose the young Japanese man while changing trains in Sendai. Without a lapse in my attention (I would like to emphasize this, as I bear a certain responsibility for him, which, under the given circumstances, is closer to obligatory supervision), he suddenly disappeared, and it is still a mystery to me how it could have happened. Now, I'm not directly to blame – when it comes down to it he's an adult and he can do whatever he so chooses to do, but I will, even if it goes against my original intention, interrupt my journey to see whether I can locate him. To save time we wanted to exclude various stations en route to Matsushima, among them Shiogama, a day's trek from Matsushima. This was where Bashō saw many historical monuments, namely the stone in the sea, Oki no Ishi, and the mountain of the ultimate pines, Sue-no-Matsuyama, both highly compelling places for a young man fantasizing about a romantic end, just as much as the picturesque cliffs in Shiogama. Around all of these places linger tales of thwarted love, meaning that – and this I mention only as *an aside – I too would consider it appropriate, all things considered, to seek them out. 'Our love will last till / over Sue's mountain of pines / Ocean waves do break.' So wrote Kiyohara no Motosuke, bringing entire generations to tears.*

At Tagajō Station, six short stops before Matsushima in the city of Shiogama, Gilbert got off the slow train on the Senseki Line and walked to Sue-no-Matsuyama.

The route took him through a completely unremarkable residential area. White low-rises up against the road, no pavement. Older residential buildings with wooden blinds at the windows, newer ones with carports and balconies, apartment blocks behind gravelled parking spaces. All things considered, just a bunch of houses squeezing themselves into narrow plots of land. There was barely enough space in the gaps between the fences and the outer walls of the buildings for a pruned, rounded conifer.

The route wasn't strenuous, but it went steadily uphill.

Low walls threw oblique rectangular shadows onto the road. Gargantuan Japanese characters were written in line-marking paint on the asphalt at junctions. The sky was spanned with drooping cables, no cars on the road, not another person in sight.

The noonday heat descended like dust and coated everything with a powdery unreality. An imposing boundary fence caught Gilbert's eye as he reached a street corner. A precast concrete wall that brought to mind narrow, vertically stacked bricks was set atop a poured concrete base drilled at equal intervals with holes to guide rainwater into the gutter, and with a chain-link fence placed on top of it. In front of this structure the road curved away toward the ultimate pines.

Soon the road narrowed to an inconspicuous footpath where three concrete barriers had been positioned to prevent cars from driving any further. At the edge of the road, at the highest point of the residential estate, were two pines, somewhat dishevelled, and nothing else. If there hadn't have been an information board, no one would have suspected this pair of pines of being anything special. Behind them, where the terrain fell away again, began a vast cemetery. Bashō mentions these graves, but it was the tree shrine that was of interest to him. He had visited the double-trunked pine of Takekuma, the dense pine grove in Sendai (which he calls the 'tree canopy'), through which no beam of sunlight could pierce, he had paid tribute to the stone in the sea overgrown with weather-beaten pines and scaled the pine mountain of Sue, one of many famous poem pillows.

The pines marked a place of classical poetry that threw up the question: what remained of the lovers after their farewell? They swore to one another that their affections would remain unchanged even during a separation, until – and here comes the rhetorical figure of impossibility – the sea's waves deluge the pine-covered peak of Sue. And as it happens, the waves of the most recent tsunamis had never reached the peak, in part because the position of the hill had, over the course of the last few centuries, shifted back a few kilometres from the shore. Nowadays, tree shrines were generally found on well-frequented roads or concreted-over squares, wizened, splitting scraps of wood people categorically need dissuading from seeing – shadows of their former selves, tainted by the bleakness of the modern age, just not worth the visit.

Gilbert carefully walked around the pines and tried to see whether he found traces of Yosa under the bushes, a suicide note, his gym bag, but when he had the sparseness of these pines before his eyes, pines that looked uncared for, neglected in spite of their status as a national cultural monument, he couldn't envisage Yosa having been there. He must have known that both of these trees, amid the banality of living, were reminiscent of the heroic and romantic past only with the aid of much good faith, and that this place was unsuitable for his purposes.

Unable to abide the pines any longer, Gilbert walked a little down the hill toward the Oki no Ishi, the stone in the sea. In the eleventh century, the court lady Nijōin no Sanuki had written a poem about unrequited love, which she compares to a stone:

> My sleeve is heavy
> and, like the stone in the sea
> that remains hidden
> even at low tide, wet and
> unbeknownst to anyone.

Gilbert quickened his steps. Why hadn't he hurried straight to the stone? Stone in the sea, doubly forsaken now that the sea had withdrawn from it too. Gilbert ran along the road. His steps pounded against it in the heat. He couldn't think straight.

He reached the multi-branched intersection out of breath. The stone in the sea was easy to spot. In place of a traffic island in the middle of a roundabout there was a fenced-off pond. Out of this pond a small island jutted up: a few boulders with three crooked pines growing from them. The rock was no longer submerged by water, it lay in a cloudy slop, which was fed by a canal inflow and might just about come up to Gilbert's knees. The concrete enclosure would allow the water to rise a further two metres, but Gilbert doubted that it would look any better at any other time of year. No sign of Yosa. Gilbert tried in spite of this to see the bottom of the pond. He shimmied all the way around the railings, green algae drifted in the water, here and there a five-yen coin winked, nothing more.

Gilbert stood pressed against the railings and jotted down a haiku, while a small truck arrived from nowhere and circled around the pool in an attempt to manoeuvre its cargo down a side street.

> On the high mountain
> where the field of graves begins
> two pines are standing

he wrote. The truck had finally found its way and turned around. The haiku was superbly executed, unpretentious and punchy. Gilbert thought it was textbook. In order to take into account the rock in the sea, he continued:

> Sea or lack thereof –
> the water here is murky,
> merely a puddle.

Then he added:

Dear rock behind bars,
please conceal yourself from me,
disappear once more!

One of the haiku he wrote for himself, the other on Yosa's behalf. Both fell somewhat short of the pine mountain haiku, they sounded mawkish and unbalanced, one could even say bleak. It wasn't all that clear to him how he should allocate these haiku. The gloomier of the haiku would be the one for Yosa or by Yosa, but the tone was similarly miserable in both. He decided to make up his mind later about which was the jolliest and then would claim it for himself. It was Yosa's own fault that hehad to be replaced by Gilbert at this point in their journey. Composing a bad poem was the lesser evil. Gilbert read the haiku through one more time, then sensed a bubbling disquiet rising up in his body, settling in his chest, bubbles bursting endlessly inside it, and he set off running, back to the train station, took the first available train, rode it three stations to Hon-Shiogama, got off, ran to the harbour, to the bay of Shiogama and its once wildly romantic cliffs.

Vast, desolate, set in concrete. The harbour basin was not made to be walked around on foot. Gilbert rushed along the edge anyway, over broad car parks from which the tourists were jammed into the boats for Matsushima, past the container warehouses, past the crane equipment, silos, mounds of grit, and white bales of compacted waste.

Time and again he thought he could see Yosa's gym bag behind a bollard on the bank, but then it would turn out to be only a rolled-up sail, a T-shirt that had been left behind, or a plastic bag.

He paced around the harbour basin in the oppressive heat for a long time, his leather bag pinned underneath his arm, dripping with sweat, thirsty, inappropriately dressed.

He had dressed like the Japanese commuters on their way to their air-conditioned offices. Dark suit, white shirt, well-polished shoes. This seemed an appropriate contemporary outfit for a travelling monk, an ascetic pilgrim; he simply blended in with the masses, even if he had had to forgo a few props that the Japanese office workforce would bring with them in the summer heat, namely a terry-cloth towel that some would drape around their necks to mop up the sweat, which usually broke out on leaving the artificially cooled rooms. Considering how honourable his enterprise was, a towel seemed too vulgar. He had read in the prospectuses lying around in the train carriages about other similar aids, special underwear that absorbed moisture in critical areas without anything being visible from the outside, and he hated to imagine that the legions of elegant men who streamed into the public transport system on a daily basis were wrapped up like babies underneath their expensive fabrics, particularly as it seemed to him that the additional layer of clothing would only make the problem worse, but that might be incorrect, seeing as the Japanese were covered up even in their leisure time – the women wore several layers of loose garments over one another, long-sleeved and short-sleeved and sleeveless T-shirts, knee-length tops over even longer skirts, all of it in sludgy or ashy tones, which, since the rekindling of the tea ceremony in this country, had been the aesthetic sensibility.

Yosa, it suddenly occurred to him, had never sweated. Yosa always appeared to be at the same temperature, lean and cool, elegant. Yosa had never been seen with such a towel. But it was possible that he had also employed certain tricks to give the impression that he wasn't a human made from flesh and blood and didn't ever perspire.

The vast harbour was completely still. No sign of unrest or excitement, no clusters of people at the edge pointing enthusiastically into the water, only wide, empty expanses of asphalt and the completely motionless sea. Gilbert slowly made his way back to the station. He sat in a small restaurant and ordered soba noodles. He was brought tea without him having asked. The word *tea* fluidly passed his lips in Japanese. He had heard Yosa use it, it seemed to have become a reoccurring motif of his project of abandonment, and so he accepted the tea without resistance, even though there were other beverages available.

He let the bowl sit there for a while so that the tea could cool, before finally leading it extremely carefully to his mouth. His face reflected in the surface of the liquid, and he looked at it more closely. It was not his face: it was Yosa's. He clearly recognized those features, the dark hair, the flatter nose, the form of the cheekbones. He swirled the bowl so that the chin with its goatee came into view. Yosa's face shyly smirked and he tried to stealthily duck to the side, but Gilbert jolted him back with the tea bowl and held him tightly in his sights. Yosa recoiled, turned his head away, closed his eyes. Then he gave up and looked Gilbert directly in the eye, subserviently, resignedly. Gilbert felt as if he was imploring him to do something, but Gilbert didn't know what. He didn't know anything anymore. He sat on a plastic stool outside a Japanese noodle bar; outside the awning the sun fell mercilessly. He had placed his leather bag on the floor between his feet and gripped it tightly with his ankles and his lower legs. He recited the poem he had written for Yosa in his head.

> *Dear rock behind bars,*
> *please conceal yourself from me,*
> *disappear once more!*

A young woman cleared away his tray. She came back with a cloth, wiped down his table, straightened the chairs. When he was sure that she wouldn't be bothering him any further, he bent back over his tea bowl. Yosa's face had gone, he only saw himself.

He didn't touch the tea. He bought two ice-cold bottles of milky, sugary isotonic water from a vending machine. He was completely dehydrated. It was possible that he'd been hallucinating. He emptied both bottles, threw them away in a trash bin in the station, and got on the train to Matsushima. Maybe Yosa had missed the connection in Sendai, perhaps he had been urged on by the crowd and sensibly stopped at the next destination, where their paths would surely cross once more. Perhaps Yosa had already gone to the pine islands.

He had sat beneath stone pines with Mathilda in Rome. Pines, whose shade they sought out time and time again, pines, whose resinous scent they inhaled, pines, tall with a cloudlike black corona. He hadn't known they were pines, they were nothing more than handy parasols to him at that point, he made use of their relative coolness, but neither he nor Mathilda were interested in conifers. Now he remembered the Jesuit-blue, the baroque-blue, the pale-blue Roman sky covered with deep black cumulus clouds. Rome, with its white towers of cloud glistening golden in its painted domes, the dark, swaying coronas of pine trees like clouds in the heavens.

The white-bearded God the Father was enthroned on the cumulus clouds, and Gilbert wandered from one church to the next with Mathilda in order to compare the depictions of God's beard. As a general rule the hair of the godly beard was wavy, it flowed down from the chin like curls of smoked eel, individual strands squirming dynamically. On the other hand, it mustn't be too fuzzy – how it flowed was imperative. The beard was white and undulating in the cloud swells of the cupolas, and this alluded to the weather god, to the weather-making power of God, but also the unseen God, who drapes himself with clouds, the unportrayable God whose countenance, even when a bold attempt is made to paint it, remains partially obscured by a flowing cloud of white. There were no alternative styles for the godly beard. The Christ figure might appear as the clean-shaven Good Shepherd as per the Roman fashion of the period; Christ Pantocrator wore a short, trimmed monarchic beard; the ailing Christ seen in gloomy baroque churches, among grinning marble skeletons and golden ossuaries and mummified popes wrapped in red velvet, shows the traditional burgeoning three-day beard, as he understandably hasn't found time in his role of the sacrificial lamb for worldly affairs such as having a morning shave. Some artists had conversely forgone tousled, unkempt hair and furnished the afflicted Christ with the so-called strategist's beard, as befitting one ready for battle. It was ultimately a conflict between heaven and hell, life and death, and it wouldn't do for the star player to be impeded by wildly flowing locks. Christ was, however, only a secondary aspect in his study. Gilbert preferred to concentrate on God the Father, whose beard wasn't, according to centuries of Christian tradition proscribing the depiction of the face of God, actually even supposed to exist.

Mathilda had been put out by this display of virility. God's beard, she had snorted, it's all about the expression and preservation of patriarchal structures, and that's all there is to it. Of course the film industry had a vested interest in it.

Mathilda gave him the feeling that the object of his study was behind the times. What about the deconstruction of traditional gender roles? What about the problematics of representation in the postmodern age? Wasn't it true that the Christian iconography of God the Father was based on Zeus and that this image persists to the present day?

After a few days Mathilda stopped accompanying him to the museums and churches, she found the glum oil paintings, the pale frescoes, the ostentatious statues all unbearable, and she was happiest when, decked out in sunglasses, summer dress, sandals, she was sitting in a piazza with a drink in front of her. For her, the Rome trip culminated in this moment, when the Roman baths, the excavated ruins, the endless ancient walls had been sightseen, when she was able to reflect upon the catacombs, the chapels, and the palazzi. Mathilda: a clearly defined body presenting herself to the sun in the Eternal City.

Gilbert often cursed himself for taking her with him. She had slowed him down, held him back in his research, deterred him from his work with her lethargy, her cultural disinterest, her disdain. She demotivated him, she made him just sit around for the second half of their trip, drinking grappa, eating ice cream, pasta, and pizza, meandering from one café to the next and yet behaving as if they were on an important mission.

Perhaps, he now thought, they should have spent more time under the pines, camped out there, looking at the horizon from the top of a hill, over the roofs and domes of the city.

And then Yosa, falling from a cliff, over and over again – he couldn't get the image out of his head, it remained unrelentingly before his eyes, imprinted over the landscape as the train chugged through it at a strangely leisurely pace, as if showing him everything one more time. Port facilities, steep coastline, the bay. They had found the optimum place, a cliff, falling majestically away, the sea very far below. Ancient pines tilting out toward the rock face, bent by storms, obstinately clinging to the hard ground, swaying in the wind. They threw a shadow that stirred and swept over the dried needles on the ground, and through this shadow slid Yosa's silhouette. He walked close to the edge, took off his shoes, fussily placed them next to his gym bag. Then he stood for a moment on the rock in thin white socks, his toes apishly curling against its surface. Gilbert wanted to call something out to him, wanted to rush over to him, grab his arm and pull him back, but his voice failed him, and for unfathomable reasons he suddenly didn't seem capable of rapid movements. He was able to advance millimetre by millimetre, as if floating; he glided out of the distance toward Yosa, he moved forward very slickly, travelling without effort, a magical wish, unfulfillable, because if he put even a minimal amount of will into his movements, if he wanted to accelerate even a tiny amount with almost imperceptible propulsion, he faltered and could go no further. He watched from a distance as Yosa jumped from the cliff. Gilbert could suddenly run again, and he sprinted, looked into the abyss, but only saw the waves far below, white, and steadily beating against the rocks. Anything that had fallen from the cliff would have hit the rocks below, but Yosa's body was already gone.

Gilbert took a step back and sat down helplessly beneath one of the gnarled trees. The cliff continued to be its windswept self, the laces of Yosa's trainers fluttered, the gym bag buckled inwards with a sucking, plasticky sound.

MATSUSHIMA

Dear Mathilda!

The pine islands of Matsushima are one of the three most beautiful landscapes in Japan. The view of them is deemed classic, inspiring, poetic. This is what makes them predestined for poetry, for utamakura, a so-called poem pillow. For centuries Japanese poets have taken pilgrimages to places of scenic allure, sought out wondrous places that are so inviting, so lovely, poems wish to settle in them. I too desired to seek out a place that so many others had visited on their travels. Matsushima, they say, is a particularly plump pillow. There are countless islands – including tiny ones – where knobbly black pines grow. The majestic pines in the Imperial Palace Gardens were pruned after their example: wind-beaten, they should look wild, as if formed by the weather and not by human hand, old pines, a symbol of endurance, solemnity, and astringency, which the wise man may be granted at the end of his life.

Japanese black pines thrive exclusively in the Japanese island kingdom and in parts of Korea. Attempts to plant them on the east coast of North America have failed: the trees were immediately infested by disease and pests and

*died. This is a coastal tree, they tolerate saltwater and can
withstand salty winds without any problem. Their wood is
the material of choice for the construction of stages for
Noh theatres because it doesn't creak.*

*Stages in Noh theatres are generally adorned with
pines and painted with pines. This is because the pine tree
functions as a site of godly manifestation. It is the earthly
site where the gods descend, which is, they say, like a light-
ning bolt coursing through a rod.*

*The Scots pine shares many qualities with the Japan-
ese black pine. It is the habitat of the Pine Beauty, the
Monk, Nun, and Pine Processionary moths, spiritual-
sounding moths, and is also a place of the eerie grand-
parental silence common to pines the world over.*

Matsushima-Kaigan. Overcast sky, silky grey and cloud-
skimmed, slim, flat clouds like the ones on Japanese folding
screens, clouds not depicted but implied by the scalloped
edges of twinkling gold leaf, highly stylized clouds, clouds
whose function amounted to making part of a landscape
vanish. The long-lost sky of a musty old postcard, the back of
it marked with greetings in old-fashioned script long since
faded into illegibility. A feeling of yellowedness hung over
Matsushima, something implausible, as if all the wanderlust
had accumulated here and could no longer find a new route
out. He had arrived at his destination. Could it be true? The
clouds that in that first moment had seemed petrified drifted
on at a brisk tempo, the wind blew cool and salty. He could
see the sea from the station.

The other passengers left the train with the bustle of locals, not troubling themselves with the view. No one apart from him had come for the pine islands.

The previous night he had lain awake for a long while and looked at the dark, restless sky. He sensed clouds swelling inside himself; they accumulated, grew to gigantic dimensions, and were set in motion by an overbearing wind. They lost their form, were torn to shreds, reconfigured themselves, changed from triumphant black to faded grey, and then became an endless grey surface, an oppressive carpet of stratus cloud from which he wanted desperately to flee, to effect an escape to that place where the clouds had their rightful place beyond his imagination: the sea.

He walked through the barrier and showed an inspector his train ticket. Then he stooped and stroked the station forecourt. He had arrived.

His journey to Matsushima had been less a matter of travelling and more a gliding or slinking, a snail-paced groping, a cloudily sedate approaching; he had travelled, it seemed to him, like a pudding, just turned out of its mould and slowly cooling, still wobbling a little, sliding helplessly down a sloping surface and losing more of its form with every amoeba-like step forward.

He stood on the windy station forecourt at Matsushima and felt a strange compulsion to his actions. A grey cumulus cloud slid over the parking bays, the dusty bushes, and the gloomy railway underpass, balling itself up over the small shops like an enormous brain – his brain.

He didn't want to submit to this impulse, and yet he did, it blew him onward like the wind did the clouds. Outwardly he seemed purposeful and ambitious, motivated if not industrious, in exactly the same way the clouds overhead seemed to strive eagerly in a particular direction, as if they had a destination in mind and had propelled themselves in its direction. For some time, however, there had been growing inside him a mistrust of this force masquerading as a motor, this impulse that he increasingly experienced as a kind of compulsion. And he sometimes wondered whether, without this compulsion, wouldn't we instead move in the same motionless way the moon moves as it rises, seemingly immutable in its tranquility, gathering all nightly things around itself?

Saigyō's journey had been guided by moonlight. It had led him through magical landscapes to solitary places, he had followed its enchantment and its beauty as he progressed farther and farther north.

Gilbert knew precisely where he wanted to go. It was a bright day, he unfolded the map showing where his reserved lodgings were, then walked through the station underpass and followed the street as it climbed more and more steeply up to his hotel.

Behind a crash barrier was a car park that, given the modest size of the town, Gilbert found to be astonishingly extensive. The car park was empty. There was a sign at its entrance: Catastrophe Assembly Point. In the event of a tsunami, one should – as Gilbert had just done – rush up the mountain, drive your car to the high-lying districts, and seek refuge from the waves in the car park. According to all human calculations, a tsunami couldn't get you here. His hotel was above the car park. As far as this matter was concerned, he would be able to sleep peacefully.

He saw himself making his way up the slope like the tiny figures following the mountain paths in the old scroll paintings, barely discernible against the stony hulks of the mountains that fill and dominate the space in these compositions, the slender figure scarcely noticeable amid the heavy brush strokes, one misplaced stroke enough to cover this delicate single line intended to represent an entire human being.

The receptionist bowed to him many times, had him sign a stack of forms, all the while conducting telephone calls in multiple languages.

No, no new guests have arrived this afternoon. No young Japanese man, no one by the name of Yosa Tamagotchi, no one under any other name, no woman, no child, no one.

The receptionist conjured up a folder of postcards, Gilbert could choose one. This game seemed rather condescending to him, but he didn't dare refuse the card. Various views of various small islands. He chose one of an island protruding starkly out of the water in the shape of a sail. This one, the receptionist noted, this one doesn't exist anymore, it was lost in the tsunami.

Gilbert politely accepted the image of the dead island with both hands.

Matsushima was beautiful, it had been for centuries – all through the centuries Matsushima had possessed the kind of beauty that even a tsunami could not harm, perhaps even the kind of beauty that could hold a tsunami at bay. The bay's countless pine-clad islands, so it was said, had mitigated the impact of the wave, had prevented something worse from happening to the surrounding area.

The receptionist led him to his room. A hotel in the Western style, no cedar-wood walls, no tatami mats or paper windows, in their place the hum of air conditioning, a reading corner, skylights that gave the sober concrete a cozy appearance, as if the sun were constantly shining into the room.

Dear Mathilda!

In his essay 'In Praise of Shadows,' the writer Jun'ichirō Tanizaki celebrates the Japanese inclination toward darkness. Recent technological advances had convinced him that his country was set on a path toward Westernization, and in the essay he expresses regret that particular aspects of traditional Japanese culture were falling to the wayside, if not completely into obscurity. For him this idea of 'Japanese' culture included a sensibility for subtle intimations, for the things that remain concealed in shadow. The West, one could pithily summarize, is bright; it not only brings with it the illumination of the Enlightenment, but also lights up every street, every town, every room with dazzling lamps, so that every single object will forevermore be sharp and delineated.

The East, conversely, prefers to allow things to emerge only vaguely from the background, to hold their mutability and fragmentariness as their defining qualities, so that it would be considered the peak of aesthetic experience to catch only a glimmer of an object. How vulgar the clearly visible object that pretends it could exist independently of its context; how glorious the twilight that strips away the substance of things, their unanswerable persuasive power, their obvious worldliness.

As a point of departure for his argument, Tanizaki took the different skin colours that prevail in the respective cultures and the different conceptions of beauty derived from them. The rosy white of people in the West is of a completely different quality to the dusky pallor of those in the East: besides his general inclination toward keeping things veiled, he sought to justify with this sleight of hand the idea that the ashen skin tone of Japanese women would really come into its own if they spent years in poorly lit homes, far from society, and then, like a ghost, with a wan face and blackened teeth, stepped out of the darkness. His conclusions are so backward, chauvinistic, and nationalistic that they gave his ideas an extremely unpleasant aftertaste. Nevertheless, the images he uses to advocate for a reduced concept of the image have a strongly sensual persuasiveness. When furnishing his new house, he wanted a bathroom in the Japanese style. He had it done out in dark wood but couldn't find an alternative for the glistening fixtures. The shining white porcelain toilet seat was particularly central in his stylistic critique. The most

*elegant solution in his eyes would be a model not available
on the market: made entirely from wood and coated with
black Japanese lacquer.*

The receptionist informed Gilbert as he walked up the stairs in
front of him that only breakfast was served at the hotel. Should
he still wish to eat, he ought to be aware that all eateries down
in the town would close at 6:00 p.m. The legs of the receptionist's trousers fell cleanly in a strange kind of slow motion right
in front of Gilbert's face. The soles of the receptionist's shoes
seemed to rise off the step only with some effort. Gilbert
walked slowly behind him; he hadn't let his small bag be taken
from him, but it seemed all the more to him that they needed a
disproportionate length of time to climb the stairs. Gilbert
leaned a little too far forward to speed up their ascent, just as
he had exercised subtle pressure on the train platform, but the
receptionist remained unaffected, raised his feet step by step
off the floor as if they were sticking to the carpet, as if one foot
were pulling up a little piece of the carpet and the stairs and
thus the entire house with it, while the other exerted a counter-
pressure and brought everything back into balance.

He had been born in Matsushima, the receptionist explained
as he opened the door for Gilbert, he had spent his entire life
here, apart from when he was studying, and never wanted to
leave again.

Shadows poured from the receptionist's sleeves, spilled
out from under the bed and the desk and submerged the
lower half of the room in a sombre vagueness, while every

object on the glossy desk provocatively took up precisely the space allocated to it, the kettle with the two upturned cups, the paper packets of sugar and tea bags, the monstrously large desk lamp with the metal shade and its movable Z-shaped arm. Only the old television seemed to hail from the same kingdom of shadows as the room itself, hulking blackly on the table, projecting into the room, and trailing a long wake of darkness behind it.

The receptionist was up to his knees in this nebulousness; Gilbert couldn't see clearly into it, and the room seemed rather dusty and the carpeted floor simply filthy, and he realized this lower part of the room was absolutely off limits and that it would be best to simply ignore it, as well as any vermin it might contain, right from the start.

While the receptionist explained all of the technical gadgetry at his disposal, as if Gilbert had never operated an electric switch before, while he praised the mosquito net over the window and stressed that one would be able to see the sea through the netting if it weren't as misty and cloudy as it was currently, Gilbert perceived the shadow sloshing around the plastic capsule of the bathroom and concentrated on the uniform folds of the grey curtains and attempted to keep up his appreciative smile throughout the entire demonstration.

He would be at reception the whole night, the receptionist said finally, full of pride. Even if someone took over his post every now and again for a couple of hours, there would always be someone to attend to Gilbert, he said as he was leaving, and it suddenly became apparent to Gilbert that no other guests were staying at the hotel.

He pictured himself for a moment wandering the corridors at night, his teeth blackened and a stiff, heavy robe of Japanese lacquer hanging from his shoulders.

Then he showered. He drank a cup of green tea. He picked up his umbrella and made his way to the bay.

Dear Mathilda,

A travel guide to the pine islands ought really to describe the route that leads to them. From an external perspective, the itinerary is easy to explain. You get on a train and you're there. The decisive question, however, is whether this route also leads to an inner understanding of the phenomenon of the Japanese black pine, so that at the end one is able to see a pine. Any decent itinerary should bring the black pine out from the void in such a way that the traveller sees before their eyes not only the pines themselves but also their infinite bifurcation back into the void, it must so enrich the traveller's experience of this abstract void with images that a sensory gateway opens up before them. Waking dreams, images that surface just before the onset of sleep when our functions of thought gradually come to rest, images that still accompany our consciousness on waking, shortly before the return of routine quotidian thought, hypnopompic hallucinations that emerge when a notion is transformed entirely into images, showing a thought in its preconceptual, not yet comprehended state, before the synthesis sets in; images, then, that must be able to accompany all my ideas, even when not everybody can always succeed in eliciting them

semiconsciously and only half-awake. Are they dreams,
daydreams, reveries? Illusions, conceits, visions? These
apparitions are said to be delusional, and yet they consti-
tute the base, the abyss of every thought, every feeling. I
wanted to cultivate the futile image of the pine from them.

Gilbert had no desire to immediately walk back down the hill he had so laboriously climbed. He avoided the road he had taken and remained for a while at the same altitude. A panoramic view. Haze in the bay, a few shapes, flecks, much of it couldn't be made out. As always, an exaggerated amount of fuss had been made over a banal landscape. From above, the islands just looked like mossy stones in the fog. Was he disappointed? He really didn't know.

Well, at least his project of abandonment had been a success. He had distanced himself from everything, as far as was humanly possible. Tokyo could be regarded as far away, and Matsushima was a good distance farther. That the young Japanese man was no longer accompanying him he took to be an advantage. From then on, no one would be able to distract him from committing his time to the pines, the moon, nature even. He had always had to keep one eye on Yosa, the boy had always been too uptight, it was impossible to ever relax in his presence, let alone concentrate on something. All hindrances to the project had disappeared in one go. Gilbert almost hoped that Yosa wouldn't reappear.

A park on the crest of a hill, lawns, benches, pines. Pines upon pines, it was almost too much for him. According to legend, Saigyō had been here and had met a young monk under the pines. This monk presented him with a kōan that he couldn't solve and, ashamed, Saigyō fled – without having reached the pine islands. Gilbert would have liked to have known what unfathomable riddle the wise travelling poet had been posed. Saigyō Modoshi no Matsu. 'The-Park-of-the-Pine-Tree-that-Sent-Saigyō-Home.' Gilbert wondered at how little it took to dissuade the celebrated pilgrims of this country from their mission. That said, the people here were hypersensitive and liable to take offence at trivialities. This, he decided, wouldn't happen to him. He would not be stopped: slight annoyances simply bounced off him, on the path of asceticism he'd chosen a little frustration was inevitable. He sat on a bench and contemplated the islands below. It was only then that he noticed the ear-piercing cicadas. They sounded electric, like an alarm system. He couldn't get the islands in his sights, they remained out of focus, veiled. It almost seemed to him that the haze was still thickening. Something began to emerge from out of the bushes – just a fox that stared at him stonily, not that that helped ease Gilbert's fear. Defenceless, he sat on the wooden bench, completely at the mercy of what was coming – not a human soul in the vicinity. The fox sniffed the air, Gilbert didn't move. Then the animal seemed to have come to an informed decision and set off, trotted past the bench, trotted past Gilbert, and disappeared between the tree trunks. Gilbert got up. The sea sparkled for a matter of seconds beneath the haze, then misted over once more. What was he waiting for? To the islands.

Gilbert found the famous Matsushima Bay installed with pontoon cranes and construction equipment. The port's defences had sustained damage during the Tōhoku earthquake; the waves had rolled over the promenade and had devastated many buildings on the waterfront. The terrain immediately behind it was steep. Overall, just as the receptionist had said, the damage in Matsushima had been limited. Construction-site fencing blocked off the front windows of a row of shops. Other shopfronts were still covered with newspaper. But a few small souvenir shops had finished their renovations and were showing off their elegant dark wooden decor and their colourful wares. Gilbert bought a fried rice dumpling at a snack kiosk. He would not eat oysters from the gravelly banks, nor seafood, nor fresh fish from the bay. Could one really know which stretches of the coast had been reached by the radioactive water from Fukushima? The hotels, huge caskets in the Japanese post-war socialist style, had remained unharmed or had already been completely rebuilt. But there was not a tourist in sight. Empty bus parks, sealed-up houses, a ghost town. He looked searchingly past the buildings covered with scaffolding and tarpaulin for a way to the beach.

The waves arched, licking the sand, melting away in white foam. They crashed against the rocks, atomized into a spray. Thin black seaweed swayed in the water, snaking around the low shoreline, and he thought of Mathilda's hair, the way it unfurled when she lay in the bath, slender eelgrass, its buoyant toing and froing.

Bashō came ashore on the island of Ojima. He came over the water from Shiogama in a rented boat and landed at Matsushima Bay in the evening with his travelling companion Sora.

Gilbert reached Ojima via a red wooden bridge. Zen monks had meditated here for decades on hard stones; this was the point of the bay at which the pine islands culminated in the mightiest of all the islands. A dirt path led along the bank, over exposed pine roots, past grottoes occupied by squatting Buddhist statues, weather-worn, encrusted with verdigris, highly dignified. Gilbert kept his distance from them, they projected a repellent greatness, a centuries-old eeriness that prevented any living being from getting too close to them. He sat beneath a tree beside the lake, leaned back against the scaly bark, and looked out over the bay.

An overhanging pine branch with black-green needles, the glittering water behind it, the islands in the evening light. From his position he could only see a part of the bay, the cluster of islands opposite blocking his view into the distance, but he wanted to stay where he was, look at the pines, wait until the moon rose above Matsushima.

That is, if the moon was going to rise at all. He hadn't the faintest idea what phase of the moon it was, full moon, new moon – his planning had really failed on this point, he had to just wait and see. Treacherous clouds might gather overhead. At that moment the sky cleared. The pines on the island opposite clung to the rocks and gently swayed in the breeze. Behind them was the deep-blue sky, the shining sea.

Thousands of needles,
thousands of kilometres
in front and behind.

It was good to lend the poems a sense of wistfulness, but on the other hand they shouldn't be too personal. He made another attempt, as unspecific as possible, as vivid as possible, trying to make the lines sound as if they had been written by Yosa.

Far away from home
pine trees as old as the stones –
fleeting clouds above.

This haiku examined the relationship between durability and ephemerality, the unremitting transitoriness of things, of travelling. He was rather taken with it and wrote on with gusto:

Screen of conifers
impenetrable shadows,
tougher than the rocks.

For Yosa he wrote:

In the fading light
waves lap against the islands,
susurrating pines.

Was he able to see? The pines, their beauty, their contours, their details, a complete picture? He didn't know where he should focus his attention: on the conifers opposite, on the bizarre rock formations protruding out of the water, on the pine branch hanging in his field of vision, which, on the one hand, was distracting, but on the other hand evoked the typical pictorial charm that he recognized from countless paintings? The view strained him. He had spent the whole day in the heat climbing asphalted-over hills, running across dreadful harbour grounds. He pressed his back against the warm bark, closed his eyes, listened to the wind running through the branches. The scent of resin. Creaking pine cones. Swishing needles. Rasping branches.

He once more closed his eyes, then closed his eyelids even tighter, sunk deeper into his exhaustion, allowed himself to be pervaded by the wind, by the scent of the pines, by the breath of the islands.

Out from the remote water of the darkness, half sleep, half dream, the overgrown rocks emerged once more, rounded like black jellyfish, brittle like dried tufts of seaweed, islands, dim silhouettes in the blackness, bubbles of darkness that held their shape, that were given a form, while behind them the darkness faded, hard cutouts over the bottomless horror, the unreasonable, furious froth. This. This is. It. Finally. Black bubbles that swirl. That burst.

He got up and wandered among the pines, between their pillowy bushels of needles, in half sleep, a fakir sleep of the constant wind. He stroked the hard black needle points, sunk them into the back of his hand to check whether or not he was in fact sleeping.

From behind the trees Yosa appeared – taller than usual, at least that's how it seemed to Gilbert – pine needles in his beard, little black needle beard, then (a tad too mischievously, at least that's how it seemed to Gilbert) Yosa bowed deeply before him. And rightly so, he thought, the young man had caused him a great deal of trouble that day, after he, Gilbert, had sacrificed his own needs again and again to take care of him.

Yosa declared that he had been dead for a long time. That he needed Gilbert to finally deliver his suicide note to his parents. He passed him a document with a Japanese inscription, which Gilbert took with both hands. His parents lived in Kanazawa. Would Gilbert be so kind as to take the letter there? His parents have been waiting for it for years. For decades. Centuries. Eternity.

A breeze made the pines shiver, and as if all the needles were falling at once, hard, fine spines, Yosa disappeared behind a curtain of murmurs, a curtain of wind. Gilbert wanted to follow him, but there was nothing there. There just wasn't anything there.

He woke up, his fists balled around dry, brown needles. The moon was over the bay, almost full, and immersing the islands in an unearthly light.

Shadow-like pine branch,
unfathomable water –
still in the moonlight.

Up the slope in the dark, beneath the street lamps, inside the booming song of the cicadas. Their spine-chilling chirping swaddled him like a cocoon, nestlike interwoven tones, a piercing ball of dried twigs that rolled with him upward, turning with every step, inevitably, against gravity, and against all reason.

It smelled of the sea and plants warmed by the sun, emanating their herby scent in the cooling evening. The hotel lobby was illuminated. Outside, through the glass door, Gilbert saw a crumpled gym bag on the gleaming stone floor. Before he could enter, the receptionist bustled over, picked up the bag, and carried it away. Gilbert stood in front of the reflective glass, looking at the cleared floor for a long time, saw his own thin reflection standing there and looking back at him. When he finally walked through the hall with unbearably loud clacking footsteps, tempestuous, troubled, no one else was there.

Back in the hotel room he switched on all the lamps, filled the kettle with water, turned on the television, the air conditioning, flicked every switch in the room as if it would mask the dreadful feeling of having been forsaken. He lay on the bed, picked up the remote control.

The news. Gale on Kyūshū. Mild earthquake in the Kansai region. A ceramics exhibition will open soon. Train delays due to a person being struck by a train. A local politician speaks into a microphone. Sumō wrestlers, practically naked, in front of a Shintō shrine. Weather forecast. Adverts. A bright red maple leaf spins over the map of Japan, it sinks down over the island of Hokkaidō and flashes nervously while green leaves pop up over the other regions, each time in places where Gilbert presumes there are the largest cities, Tokyo, Ōsaka, Hiroshima, Kanazawa, comically drawn leaves, thickly outlined, kimono patterns, teapot decorations.

Last year's autumn depicted in fast forward, red maple foliage making its way from north to south, from the coasts to inland, from the mountains to the flatlands, bright red leaves sweeping in a wave over the country, leaving behind a faded yellow where the foliage had peaked and had in truth not yellowed but fallen.

A photo from today to end on: red foliage in front of a river at the northernmost point of the country. Travel tips for the Ashikawa region, where brown bears roam through forests and it's not all that far to the Russian island of Sakhalin. Red leaves, a complementary red for all the things in this country that stay green. The bamboo. The pines. The tea.

It would be unthinkable to make a special trip just for a tree back home, just for some leaves! The Japanese maple with its filigreed leaf takes on a carmine red like the American sugar maple when a period of sunny, mild days and cold, frosty nights sets in in the autumn. Japanese television has daily reports about the progress of the changing of the leaves, and a great number of enthusiasts pay attention to this information and set forth, travelling on to the next location. In the past few days Gilbert had become used to the idea of undertaking trips to marvel at trees, a completely useless custom that remained deeply enrooted in Japanese culture. It wasn't an educational journey in the European sense, one that could be bragged about for many years to come, like when one travels to Rome and will always be a person who has seen the Sistine Chapel, the Colosseum, the baths, the portrait of Innocent X. This viewing of natural phenomena was linked neither with art nor with architecture, nor with history; it was tender and mysterious, and if a form of education were to come from it, it was impossible to explain or recall afterward.

Now he saw a deciduous tree, which, like a nightmare, would turn red overnight. All its leaves fall off one after the other, and the tree stands there bare. Without savouring the cardinal-red adornment, the flames, the play of colours. Without following the orderly sequence of the leaves, without him seeing most of them landing in a brook and being carried away by the water. Some get entangled in the overgrown riverbank, some stay hanging from a rock, quivering on the stones, come free and keep going.

Gilbert turned off the television. He made the tea, turned out the lights, walked over to the window. Outside, more grotesque branches in the secretive moonlight.

Plant shadows wandered over the wall, staggered noiselessly through the room, swept over the far end, then froze. They paused, skipped the bedsheet, then swung on further, brushed against his cheeks, washed over him, thinned twigs that touched everything too tenderly for Gilbert to bear. A forest of waifs, disembodied wood, a grey pyre built of shadows. He heard the wind in the pines, heard their monumental whirring, the anti-wood on his wall rose and fell, a long, lonely wandering, and yet … He stood at the window, holding the teacup with both hands. It caught the moon for an instant. Macaques cackled far off in the distance.

Mathilda wasn't a big fan of conifers. She particularly loathed sparse firs, the kind older homeowners used to border their gardens, an impenetrable dark wall from inside the property, rigorously trimmed from the outside so that not a single twig jutted onto the pathway. For passersby there is only the sight of the bare reverse, the sight of snags with dried brown needles stuck to them.

Mathilda had two more days of teaching, then it would be the weekend, and then the autumn holidays would begin.

He would call her, he told himself. Mathilda, sweetheart, he would say. Let's meet in Tokyo, he made a mental note, it's all very simple, come meet me in Japan. The leaves are starting to turn.

ACKNOWLEDGEMENTS

The author and translator would like to acknowledge the German and English translators of Bashō and Saigyō – Geza S. Dombrady, David Landis Barnhill, and those uncredited – whose work was used as reference to create versions of the haiku and tankas that appear in this book.

ABOUT THE AUTHOR
AND TRANSLATOR

Marion Poschmann was born is Essen in 1969. Recognized as one of Germany's foremost poets and novelists, she has won both of Germany's premier poetry prizes. She is the author of four novels, three of which have been nominated for the German Book Prize, and she won the prestigious Wilhelm Raabe Literature Prize in 2013. *The Pine Islands* is her first novel to be translated into English.

Jen Calleja is a writer and literary translator from the German. She was shortlisted for the 2019 Man Booker International Prize for her translation of *The Pine Islands* and the 2018 Schlegel-Tieck Prize for her translation of Kerstin Hensel's *Dance by the Canal*. She is the author of *I'm Afraid That's All We've Got Time For* (Prototype, 2020).

Typeset in Arno.

Printed at the Coach House on bpNichol Lane in Toronto, Ontario, on Zephyr Antique Laid paper, which was manufactured, acid-free, in Saint-Jérôme, Quebec, from second-growth forests. This book was printed with vegetable-based ink on a 1973 Heidelberg KORD offset litho press. Its pages were folded on a Baumfolder, gathered by hand, bound on a Sulby Auto-Minabinda, and trimmed on a Polar single-knife cutter.

Cover design by Ingrid Paulson
Designed by Crystal Sikma

Coach House Books
80 bpNichol Lane
Toronto ON M5S 3J4
Canada

416 979 2217
800 367 6360

mail@chbooks.com
www.chbooks.com